BIG MOJO

ALSO BY JACK GETZE

Austin Carr Mysteries
Big Numbers
Big Money

JACK GETZE

BIG MOJO

Down & Out Books
3959 Van Dyke Rd, Ste. 265
Lutz, FL 33558
www.DownAndOutBooks.com

Cover design by JT Lindroos

ISBN: 1937-4957-6-0

ISBN-13: 978-1-937495-76-3

For Angelina, Grace, Kyleigh and James

ONE

The big thing about Jersey stockbrokers: we're in a cutthroat occupation. If we don't keep our client names and their contact information secure, other brokers will pirate our business. In a room full of telephone salesmen, somebody is *always* switching firms, stealing every name and phone number they can duplicate. Thus, when my associate and former boss Vic Bonacelli calls, asks me to step into his office and meet one of his customers, I'm stunned. And since I closely watched a smoking hot redhead strut inside Mr. Vic's private spaces not ten minutes ago, my curiosity quickly displays itself in a feverish sweat.

When Mr. Vic originally founded our Jersey Shore broker-dealer securities company thirty-five years ago, the firm could accept cash in payment for municipal, tax-free bearer bonds. Taking advantage of this fact, Mr. Vic's first customers tended to be tax cheats—boardwalk vendors and other small business types who collected lots of cash, and whose personal constitutions prevented them from paying Uncle Sam full tribute.

By recognizing the vulnerability therein, let's call it a Quixotic focus on political principal, Mr. Vic easily skimmed ten percent from such cash transactions. He did it so happily, and with such charm, three decades later ninety percent of all those early clients—or their surviving children—still do business with him. Put more succinctly, Mr. Vic still has a lot of crooks on the book.

My name's Austin Carr, by the way, President of Carr Securities, Inc., Members of the American Association of Securities Dealers. Though I refuse to rob our customers like Mr. Vic used to, I had hoped my fifty-one percent ownership in the recently renamed Carr Securities would provide for my children's university education. Currently, however, Bob the Dentist—my ex-wife's boyfriend—seems a more likely candidate. Carr Securities is barely running in the black, and my only real income these days is commission on my personal stock and bond sales.

I knock on Mr. Vic's closed office door.

"Come on in, pal," he says.

Mr. Vic's spaces have returned to their original, antique, fox-and-hounds, boy-are-we-old-money glory. Hard to do in Jersey, but Vic tries. While he and his wife were in Italy last year, Vic leaving me to hold a large empty bag for him, I occupied the big office in a more Spartan manner. In the interest of peace and hoped for harmony—our one-office firm needs Vic's sales production—I let him have his big office back despite having wrestled control of the company from him.

His fancy liquor cabinet was empty anyway.

Vic saying, "Patricia, I'd like you to meet my partner, Austin Carr. Austin, this is Patricia Willis."

Dressed for a Jersey fox hunt, Ms. Patricia Willis shines summer eyes at me—iris the color of reflected sky on shallow water. Her shoulder-length ginger hair fits perfectly around her oval face, her figure shows off womanly curves, but it's her knockout blue eyes that hold my stare. My heart flickers, in fact. Easy, boy. I've seen Patricia Willis visit Mr. Vic's office before, and my married junior partner is notorious not only for his infidelities, but for stabling multiple girlfriends at the same time. Still, it won't be easy keeping my eyes off Ms. Patricia Willis. My interest in fiery-haired women goes back to *I Love Lucy* reruns and Lucille Ball. It's practically genetic.

Wonder why Vic has the radio on?

Patricia says, "Nice to meet you, Austin."

I give her the full-boat Carr grin. "You, too, Ms. Willis."

The redhead's smile twists into an odd smirk. My blood pressure creeps higher. Taking in her Trollop of the Stables dress code—tight suede riding pants, black leather boots and a white, low-cut blouse—I'm guessing Patricia knows how to spend quality time on her own back, not just a horse's.

"Patricia just told me quite a story," Vic says.

I stifle a choke.

"A story I think you should hear," he says.

Oh, boy. I love stories.

When Patricia stops talking four minutes later, I slouch back in Mr. Vic's red leather armchair and let the soft jazz on the Bose play deeply on my neck and shoulders. Now I know why my partner has the radio on. He hopes the music will calm him. I know *my* heart's thumping hard rock boogie after the redhead's tale. Boy could I make a boat load of money. Money I need badly for Beth and Ryan's college education. But getting caught profiting on inside information—she's got it, the real thing—means losing Carr Securities and my securities license. Not to mention the public disgrace. Imagine what my kids would go through at school.

Imagine what I'd go through selling used cars.

Mr. Vic stares at my tie like I spilled mustard on it. He's not always a bad guy, but right now he believes Patricia's info gives him a winning lottery ticket. His black greedy eyes and pinched brow don't care about my family's future, just his own.

"So, what do you think?" he asks. "Is a story Patricia heard from her brother really inside information?"

I stare back at him like Vic's the mustard. Could Vic really *not* know Patricia possesses true inside information? It should be obvious to any securities professional. Maybe I misunderstood something.

My gaze shifts back to Patricia, successfully avoiding her large and available cleavage. Not an easy trick, even with the red hair as an alternate attraction. "Before I answer Vic's question, let me make sure I have this straight, Ms. Willis. Your brother, a big shot Manhattan attorney, is working on a merger agreement between Fishman Corporation and Gene-Pak Industries; that is, your brother is helping negotiate and prepare—actually write the legal merger documents. Is that correct?"

"Yes."

"And this merger has yet to be publicly announced?"

"Yes," she says. "Like I just told you. My brother said Gene-Pak will pay at least forty dollars a share for Fishman stock—maybe more if the market goes up."

Fishman currently sells at thirty-two. Part of my brain—the greedy, Mr. Vic part—has already done the math, and believe me, if I picked the right stock option, I could make four or five times my money on a deal like this. Put up fifty grand, get back a quarter million.

The soft jazz helps, but my pulse is still too fast.

I glance back at Mr. Vic. "Information doesn't *get* any more inside than this. Her brother the attorney signed confidentiality papers he apparently hasn't read. If he gets caught *talking* about this merger, he's finished as a lawyer. If he gets caught giving out the information, he'll be disbarred."

Patricia says, "How would they ever catch him—or us?"

Us? "Your brother will be on a list of lawyers and other people who have prior knowledge. The exchanges and the Securities and Exchange Commission keep track. They'll check his accounts if suspicious trading turns up in the stock. Is his name the same as yours—Willis?"

"Yes," the redhead says.

"Then when the New York Stock Exchange computers look at all the people who purchased stock and options before the merger, your name will pop up in red caps. And so will anyone else who bought Fishman, has the name Willis or lives in Branchtown. The computer figures you might know them."

"But only if there's an investigation of unusual trading, right?" Vic says. "The SEC doesn't do it automatically with every merger deal. If she doesn't get too greedy, the stock doesn't exceed its normal volume, maybe they don't notice, right?"

"It's possible," I say. "But very risky with the same name."

"Maybe what Patricia wants to know," Vic says, "is what's the worst that could happen? If she gets caught, doesn't she just say I'm sorry and give the money back?"

I stare at Patricia. "If you get caught, your brother gets disbarred, maybe prison. You might also pay double your profit in fines. And if you tell one little lie about your involvement first—try to hide the truth and keep the dough like Martha Stewart—well, Ms. Willis, you are possibly on your way to prison."

"What if I open a bank account in the Cayman Islands?" Patricia says.

I sigh, lean back and signal Vic with an eyebrow. This redheaded hottie is *his* client, probably a girlfriend. She has to trust him pretty darn well to tell him about her brother and this merger deal, then let him bring me into the room. Come on, Mr. Vic, take Patricia Willis to the 'splaining department.

"What about it?" Vic says to me. "The Caymans?"

Not exactly the words I wanted to hear, partner. I shrug. "The Cayman banks might keep their mouths shut. They say Panama's better. But I'm not getting involved in this. And neither is my firm."

"*Our* firm," Vic says.

"I control the stock now, not you."

"Fifty-one to forty-nine."

"Ask J. Paul Getty's heirs about the significance of fifty-one percent," I say. "But why don't you and Patricia fly to Panama City this weekend, take your checkbook and credit cards with you, go crazy buying Fishman options. I'm not risking it, and neither is this firm."

Pulling myself out of the red leather armchair, I step nearer Mr. Vic. "In fact, I don't even understand why you asked me to hear this story."

My partner works his lips, but he doesn't speak. At least not now.

I turn to the redhead. "Is this story even legit?"

Her chin lifts half an inch. The cleavage rises with it. "*Every*thing about me is legit."

TWO

Back on the trading desk, my pulse leads the Kentucky Derby. Real inside information. I don't think people outside the securities business can understand or appreciate what this means to a stockbroker. Sure we spend five days a week telling our customers which stocks are going up and which ones are headed down. But it's all baloney. Nobody can predict the future.

Especially stockbrokers from Jersey.

"What are you so excited about, Carr? I haven't seen you glassy-eyed like this since Ryan hit that walk-off home."

The pest over my shoulder—the guy talking about my son the Little Leaguer—is Bobby G, former sales-floor cohort, now my employee. His bed head, bushy red hair could be mistaken for a rusty mop, which is fitting because Bobby sucks up gossip like the best floor sponge.

"Come on, what's the story?" he says.

"Yeah," Carmela says from the trading desk. "What did that bimbo tell you and my father?"

"Nothing good." I lie.

Carmela runs our trading department. She's Mr. Vic's oldest daughter. Not all the employees of Carr Securities have adopted a proper new tone and manner toward me, one that reflects my recently increased ownership. In Bobby G's case, this is because he and I share tequila and tacos at least once a week during Little League baseball season. Our sons play on the same team. Carmela's attitude is hard to gauge, let alone explain.

I click my computer screen off a chart of Fishman and try the general business news section. "Vic's redhead had a question about interest rates," I say. "It was nothing."

"BS, Carr," Bobby G says. "You're blushing. You got a tip, didn't you?"

Oh, boy, did I. I have to take deep breaths, cut back on this emotional, girlish excitement. Men are supposed to remain calm in the face of a potentially huge financial gain. Not that I'd ever risk buying stock on inside information.

Ever, ever, ever.

I stand up, my shoulder brushing Bobby G's. "I'm going to lunch."

Bobby says, "Fishman, huh? What's up with that old dog?"

Inside Luis' Mexican Grill, chatter, laughter, and a serious background buzz of sustained chew-and-chomp attack my eardrums. Chef Umberto waves at me through the kitchen doorway. The air smells of cilantro and fresh corn tortillas. Not much symbolic of Jersey at Luis', unless you count beer consumption and fleshy faces.

On the way here, I thought seriously about what might be best for my two children, Ryan and Beth. I was thinking, specifically, maybe I should, in fact, be risking disgrace, the business and my stockbroker license.

No, no, no. I'm not really going to do it. I was just letting Mr. Greed have his say. But here's what Mr. Greed was thinking: If I rounded up all the cash I could, borrowed from my aunt and uncle's small trust account I manage, then flew to Panama, used the money to buy Fishman stock options, I could make two-fifty or three hundred thousand dollars profit on Patricia Willis' inside information. Enough money, if invested right, to pay for the combined eight years of education at just about any university Beth *and* Ryan could choose.

The heart of all investment decisions is the fear versus greed equation, and sometimes I think the equation applies to everything in life. Is it worth the risk to take care of my children's future?

No. I'll find another way.

Behind his huge horseshoe bar, my friend and establishment owner, Luis Guerrero, waves a strange hello at me while serving green margarita snow cones to a group of middle-aged housewives, a foursome fresh off the municipal golf course. I've seen the same group here before. They like to perch and eat at the bar so Luis serves them. And why not? Luis is dashing and handsome, a thin and muscled foreigner in a world of overfed electricians, plumbers, bankers and horse players. But too bad, ladies. My favorite bartender, sage, hombre and club owner, Luis Guerrero, gets married this weekend. In fact, tonight's the rehearsal dinner and I'm invited.

Oops. There's Tom Ragsdale—Rags we call him—my former sales manager when Carr Securities used to be called Shore Securities. He's at Luis' bar, tucked back in a dark shadow under the ceiling-suspended television set. Hiding like a bat. I don't think his eyes are *really* glowing. It's probably that I hate him so much. I can't believe he's here. That odd wave Luis gave me earlier must have been a warning.

I choose a stool as far from Rags and the golf ladies as Luis' bar will comfortably allow and wait for my friend. When Luis finally visits, I order a shot of Herradura, a tequila made popular by Hollywood screenwriters last century, and still my favorite liquor produced from cactus. Or succulents. Whatever blue aguave plants are.

"Let's toast your wedding," I say.

"Perhaps you should show your enthusiasm in a manner less alcoholic," Luis says. "You must be coherent, alert even, for the rehearsal tonight. Father Ignacio will be disturbed if you pass out or vomit during his instructions."

In the corner of my eye, Rags leaves his drink and comes zipping around the curved bar like a terrain-tracking missile. Clearly, the pointy-nosed little rodent is headed my way. Crap. The guy is not only mean, stupid and boring, he also hates me. In a rage, Rags once hit me with his moving Jaguar.

"Perhaps a beer?" Luis says.

Luis likes to show people the proper path. I think maybe it's because he's descended from Toltec warriors. Even in his bartender uniform—black slacks and white dress shirt with the sleeves rolled up, showing off his Popeye muscles—Luis' European features don't hide the Native American in his ancient hunter's gaze.

Rags saunters up, filling the empty spot beside my stool. He smells like a cigarette butt. I forgot how beady his dirt-colored eyes are, how quickly they shift from side to side. I give Rags the Rat a half-boat grin. I'm democratic that way. "What's up, Rags? Haven't seen you for a while."

"I want my stock back," he says.

Rags refers to the seventeen percent interest in the former Shore Securities I bought from him last year when he and Carmela were having an on-again, off-again, on-again divorce. Carmela's dad Mr. Vic sold Rags the stock while they were married. I took the stock off Rags' hands cheap while they were getting divorced.

"Carmela hasn't mentioned you two getting back together," I say. "But hey, you want the stock, fine. Just hand me a cashier's check for three-hundred thousand." My purchase price was less than five percent of that figure. At the time, our firm was generally thought to be circling bankruptcy.

Rags bangs his fist on the bar.

I shift my gaze to his hands so I'll see the punch coming. He has to be pissed. Carmela says he's lost everything, says he works now in some kind of giant bakery or factory up in northern Jersey.

"Am I making you nervous, Carr?" he says.

"You did cream me once with a foreign substance."

It takes Rags three or four seconds to figure out I mean his Jaguar. "Too bad I wasn't going faster."

I peek at Luis' ornamental sombreros overhead. A row of these wide-brimmed *caballisto* hats hang all around the horseshoe bar. I'd never tell Luis, but the setup is quite reminiscent of hub caps at a junk yard.

"Killing you then would have saved me a whole lot of trouble," Rags says.

When I glance again at my former sales manager's hands, I notice there's a gun in one now—the left, I think, although it's taking my brain a while to confirm. My nerves are engulfed in a cold polar vortex. I have to admit Rags is scaring me. He's crazy enough to shoot. He holds the weapon low, on his hip, with his sport coat shielding the small automatic from Luis' patrons. Rags says, "You've *always* been a pussy, you know that?"

I'm waiting for the shot. Waiting for the pain to rip through my gut. This crazy son-of-a-bitch has been my enemy since the day he came to work at the old Shore Securities. He was Mr. Vic's future son-in-law then, a pain in *every*body's ass. But he was always a long hard stick up mine.

Rags' jaws tense. He leans forward, inching the pistol's muzzle closer to my heart. "One way or the other," he says, "I'm getting—"

I follow Rags' worried gaze toward whatever has distracted him.

It's Luis, my friend and favorite all-time greatest bartender, sliding a waded towel across the bar toward Rags. I don't see how a towel is going help much until the black business end of a large caliber pistol peeks from the soiled material. Luis' interruption comes to rest inches from Rags' ribcage, the bartender's forefinger pressing against a strategic spot in the towel.

Luis is all smiles. "Please lay your weapon gently on top of my bar, near this rag."

None of us move. I'm sure my nutty ex-sales manager is going to kill me. The restaurant presses on, oblivious and noisy while Rags seems to think over his situation in more detail. What's to think? Is he going to shoot me or not? You would expect the man to do what Luis says, guns being pointed the directions they are now, the look on Luis' face. But I know Rags is crazy enough to shoot anyway, take a bullet from Luis. Inside my cold skin, a frightened heart beats mambo time.

Luis leans closer to Rags. "If I am successful in targeting your spine, this forty-four magnum will cut you in equal halves."

Rags works his jaw like he's chewing gum. One beat. Two. Finally air hisses between his teeth. Submission. He takes his finger off the trigger, slides the lady-size automatic onto the bar beside the towel.

I take my first breath in thirty seconds.

Luis waves his bartender wipe-cloth like a magician—one swipe and everything disappears below his bar.

Luis and I glare silently at him until Rags takes an angry first step toward the front door. But he stops and turns. "One way or the other, Carr, I'm getting the stock back. And I'm not the only one who wants what you took."

"Oh yeah? Who?"

"Mr. Vic and his mother, for starters."

"Mama Bones?" I say. "Are you kidding? She *loves* me."

THREE

Ignoring her cell phone chimes—bells recorded for her at the Vatican—Mama Bones Bonacelli slips the old skeleton key into the lock. A twist, a familiar click, and the half-ton basement door glides open with a gentle push. Aunt Maria's old bronze and wrought iron entry swings easy now that Gianni installed those six barrel hinges with ball bearings and grease fittings. Mama Bones can get inside her hideaway smooth and fast now, quicker even than her dead husband Domenic in bed. Ha.

Inside, Mama Bones flips the new light switch. Overhead fluorescents blink on one at a time, clicking and clacking like cans of tomatoes rolling off a cupboard shelf. She shuffles across the newly refurbished second kitchen, her sneakers pushing ripples on the dirt floor. Her husband Domenic wanted to lay tile down here when they bought the place thirty years ago. He was from California and didn't understand about second kitchens in the basement—where Italian families like Mama Bones' killed chickens, boiled and preserved bushels of peppers and tomatoes, or cooked up forty, fifty quart jars worth of red gravy for freezing. Enough food to last a winter.

"You gotta have the dirt down here, Domenic," she whispers now, three decades later. "Notta the fancy tile."

Domenic. She doesn't miss or talk to him much anymore. He's been dead too long. She is too busy. But now, with her own comfortable space down here to sit and remember the past, who knows. Maybe she'll bring down that picture of Domenic from upstairs, the one of him in the tux, set him on one of the olive oil barrels.

Ignoring the phone again, she opens the giant Kenmore refrigerator, reaches for an opened jug bottle of Gallo Brothers Paisano. Nice boys, those Gallo Brothers. So are Gianni and Tomas nice brothers, Mama Bones' nephews who fixed up her old basement this summer. All new appliances, the refinished table with a desktop computer, electricity, a clean new pallet for her jugs of olive oil, drawers for her gang's hand-written-only revenue and expense books. And now today, with those six new hinges, Mama Bones can get in and out of here easy. Do some cooking, have a glass of California wine, even play with Aunt Maria's old book of magic spells for fun. Relax a little. This is the new Mama Bones' private getaway. And who knows, maybe she'll have time to talk again to her ex-husband Domenic.

Probably not much, though. He was a mean son of a bitch.

Her cell rings again. These new telephones, you can see who's calling, decide if you want to talk to the person or not. Oh, Vic again. Her son really gets himself worked up about Austin Carr, that Carr Securities sign on Vic's old place of business. Wonder what happened with her son's big insider trading scheme. Said he was going fix things.

Mama Bones pours a glass of wine, sits down at the nice round table Gianni and Tomas bought her. Smooth dark wood. Her handsome nephews treat her well. Whereas her son, Vittorio, or Vic, not so much.

"'Allo, Vic. What'sa the matter now?"

"Oh ditch the accent, Ma. You don't have to pretend you're stupid with me."

"You sure? I want to make the conversation easy for you."

"Ha ha."

"Ha, yourself. What do you want, huh? You been calling all day."

"You know why I'm calling. We've waited months, like you said. Tell me why you won't take care of the guy who's torturing me."

She swallows a mouthful of wine, clears her throat. "I'm not asking for a hit on Austin. He doesn't deserve it. He didn't do nothing bad. Truth is, Austin's smarter at business than you. You left the country, remember? You left Austin all alone to deal with Bluefish. His friends took care of it, too. The place would belong one hundred percent to New York if it wasn't for Austin. So why you want to kill him?"

She can hear through the phone her son don't like what she's saying. Too bad. The truth hurts.

"This is *our* stock and bond business," Vic says. "You and Daddy helped me start Shore Securities thirty-five years ago. You going to let some big mouth, fast-talking prick like—"

"Watch your mouth."

Vic sighs like a girl. "Okay, forget about having him killed. Talk to him. Rough him up some, explain he has to sell me back Carmela's and Walter's stock at a fair price."

Mama Bones sips her wine. "I thought you were going to set him up for insider trading. You know, get rid him that way. Cost him his Series Seven license."

"I could, and maybe still will, but I'd rather not. It would be a lot easier—and a lot more profitable—if my Austin Carr problems went away so I could use Patricia's information all for myself."

"Listen, you want Austin beat up, you do it. But you'd better watch out. The man is trickier than Bugs Bunny. You try to push him over a cliff, you'll end up with a giant carrot up your ass. Who knows what it'll cost you this time."

"What do you mean?"

"I have to spell it out? You left him to deal with Bluefish, he ends up with a majority share of the company."

"Jeez, Ma. Why do you talk like that to me? You want Austin to steal *all* of our business? How do *you* feel when you see that giant Carr Securities sign Sunday when you go to church?"

Mama Bones sets down her wine, opens the three-holed notebook centered on the round table—her collection of Aunt Maria's spells. "Okay, Vic, I tell you what. I gotta an idea that maybe will help. We'll have some laughs with Austin, get him in trouble. How's that sound, huh?"

"No magic spells, okay? Gianni told me the way you've been fooling around with your aunt's magic again. Reading that book of hers. He says it makes the crew wonder if you've got all your marbles."

Holding the phone to her ear, Mama Bones searches the shelves near the table, checking the contents of one dusty cigar box after another, then a series of sealed ceramic jars.

Various ingredients for Aunt Maria's recipes stare back at her, offering memories and smells from the past. Lavender. Garlic. Unborn mice. Finally, her fingers pinch inside a jar of cranberry pits.

"Don't you worry," she says. "This'll work."

It's true the magic Mama Bones learned from her Great Aunt Maria often fails. So far the potions have offered what Vic, the smarty pants, calls a "low rate of return." But *this* time, Mama Bones is pretty sure the magic spell is going to work great. Past performance indicates success. Ha.

"Ma?" Vic says. "No magic, okay? Promise me."

"You wanna make a bet this potion works?"

"Oh, jeez. No, no, no. Please."

"You wanna bet it works or not?"

Vic sighs again like a girl. "O-kay. Five thousand says Austin Carr doesn't feel a thing. Whatever it is you give him."

"Make it *twenty* grand, smarty pants. I wrote down the ingredients for *this* spell extra carefully fifty-two years ago, and it already worked once. I was a teenager, and guess what I wanted? What do *all* teenage girls think about, huh?"

FOUR

I'm not sure the black silk cummerbund is on correctly, but, boy, do I look good in a tux. Right out of *Esquire Magazine.* Austin Carr will be a hit at the wedding reception—the ladies will go nuts. As all men eventually realize, dressing like flightless birds is one of the easiest ways to tap female illusions about civilizing men.

I am honored to be in Luis' wedding party. Of the five ushers, I'm the only one who wasn't born south of the border. Austin Carr, token gringo. Although being born and raised in Los Angeles should count for something. L.A. used to be part of Mexico, and is still the second-largest city in the world where the majority of the citizenry speak Spanish.

Parking the Camry, my gaze catches Luis' friend and restaurant chef, Umberto, leaving the snappy-dressed group of ushers roosting on the church steps. Looks like Umberto is headed my way. Bushy wild hair and a mouth as big as a pablano chili; but even Umberto looks good in a tux. Like a freakish James Bond villain.

I slide into the late morning sunshine. St. Theresa's rests only a block from our offices in downtown Branchtown, and I can hear the minor hiss of weekend traffic mixing in with the echo of musical church bells. Dead perennial hibiscus stalks, a reminder of summer, form a tan row beside a line of green privet.

Umberto digs inside his coat pocket for something, and shows me on arrival: It's a black and white photograph, a candid, magnified head-and-shoulders of a tough-looking Hispanic male, a shot you might see in the post office on the FBI's Most Wanted list. Yikes. Late thirties or early forties, with a devilish mustache, a pointed goatee and tortured Native American nose. The tattoo on his neck is a skull and crossbones.

"Who's this?" I say. "The priest?"

"This is not a joke," Umberto says. "This man is *muy malo*, very bad. He comes here from Luis and Solana's past, threatening to prevent a marriage he believes insults his love for Solana. We must all of us watch for him. He was spotted near the train station last night."

"I don't understand?" I say. "He's an old boyfriend of Solana's?"

Umberto shrugs. "He is Santo Vargas. Watch for him."

I worry for a while about Mr. Vargas, but when the wedding music starts, I'm the first one down the aisle. Well, me and Jessica, a petite blonde whose big puffed up hairdo barely reaches the top of my cummerbund. Such a dainty little thing, tiny Jessica. When I met her last night at the rehearsal dinner, I thought she was the ring-bearer.

"Step on my dress like you did last night," Jessica says, "I'll kick you in the balls."

Maybe dainty isn't the right word.

No sign of any trouble, the ceremony goes off perfectly. Luis and Solana flee the church under clouds of thrown flower petals, the bags waiting for us in baskets near the big church doors. We'll see the couple later at a hotel reception, but for now the crowd on St. Theresa's marble steps is happy to watch the couple drive off, then trade handshakes, hugs and kisses. It's a friendly crew, and though I make a gregarious and rousing start at engagement, shaking enough hands to get elected Branchtown Mayor, I soon must slip away for a restroom.

Too much wine last night. Too much coffee this morning.

A knowledgeable source in a black and white habit directs me through various turns in the hallway behind the last church pew, and I find the men's with little trouble. On the way inside, I notice the broad, muscular back of a guy standing near the entrance, and after I pass him, I sense his energy coming inside behind me. But I don't realize quickly enough he means me harm.

A kick smacks my spine below the shoulder blades, the powerful force knocking me forward, expressing my weightless body into the bathroom. I get my hands up but still collide head-first with the wall of a stainless steel toilet compartment. Stars and planets circle my stunned consciousness. My legs fold, dropping me onto the tile floor. My hands press against the cold wetness. I shiver in disgust. A minty sweet disinfectant doesn't hide the aroma of fresh urine.

Hands grab my tuxedo. They leave me sitting, but slam my head against the steel again. Adrenaline pumps my vision back, and I focus on the man crouched over me. A Native American face, but without the feathers or wisdom. I haven't met a smart guy yet wore a skull and crossbones tattoo on his neck.

This is Santo Vargas. Not quite the same—no beard and 'stash—as Umberto's picture, but close enough.

"Where will Solana go on her honeymoon?" he asks.

Vargas' face and tattoo are intimidating, but his eyes are like nothing I've ever seen. More purple than hazel, they are gemstones embedded in the dark brown face of a prison-hardened First American.

His fist pummels my left temple. Once more my head bangs against the stall. The stars and planets turn into red shooting comets.

"Where will Solana—"

"The Martha Washington," I say. "Luis and Solana are staying above the reception tonight."

Vargas seems skeptical. Could be his black and brooding eyebrows that make me think that. Or maybe it's the switchblade he's withdrawn from his back pocket.

Click. Extended, the turquoise-handle weapon is as long as a barbecue fork. The double-edged tip touches my nose. "If this is not the truth," he says, "I will cut out your eyes."

"There's a room key in my coat pocket," I say. "I'm supposed to give it to Luis at the reception."

Vargas reaches his scarred claw of a hand inside my tuxedo coat pocket. His fingers probe my ribs like pliers, then wrap around the credit card that passes for a hotel key. The room number—233—is penciled on the paper envelope protecting the key card, but I'm not giving up Luis and Solana. I rented 233, my own junior suite above the reception, in case I get lucky with one of the bridesmaids tonight—anyone but Jessica.

"Luis asked me to get the room in my name," I say. "They're going to drive away, then sneak back later."

Hope I'm still a good liar. Vargas' movements are deliberate, exaggeratedly so, like a robot the way he assesses the hotel key. The number. The paper. The magnetic strip on the card. Seems like a full minute before he looks down at me again with those odd Tyrian purple eyes. "I wonder why you would so easily give up your friend," he says. "One who trusts you to hold this key for him."

I push up from the tile floor. He doesn't object, but the tip of Vargas' switchblade tracks my nose as I rise. Fighting dizziness, I hold the stall for balance. My forehead pounds—a lump is rising. If I yelled, would anyone hear me?

"Why do you betray him?" Vargas says. "Answer me."

I freeze as Vargas' knife touches my neck. My heart thumps like a rabbit's. What I say next will sound like the truth because I absolutely believe it. "I'm not betraying him. Luis beats guys like you with one hand."

Vargas smiles. "I have defeated Luis before. I could do so again."

He flips his back on me and strides away. His reminds me of a larger version of Luis, the quickness of his feet, the shift of his broad shoulders.

"You will of course tell Luis I am coming," he says.

FIVE

Luis and Solana's noisy wedding reception fills the Martha Washington Hotel's fanciest riverside ballroom. The walls are floor to ceiling windows, and a high-ceiling showcase for the picturesque Navasquan River and Branchtown's waterside cafes and shops. The afternoon light shines spectacularly on the water, our mood happy and festive.

I lift my champagne glass high for a one-on-one toast with Luis' cook Umberto. We are both in line to officially greet the new couple, shake Luis' hand and kiss the bride. Earlier, I told Luis what happened with Santo Vargas.

"To Luis and Solana," I say to Umberto. "To their happiness."

New Jersey's best enchilada-maker clinks my glass with his, but Umberto's dark brown eyes focus on the spreading lump of purple across my forehead. "Happiness for Luis and Solana, *si*," the chef says, "but tell me what you have told Luis. It was Santo Vargas who gave you this beating, was it not? He was seen minutes ago in the parking lot."

I sip my champagne, check out the crowd. "I wouldn't call it a beating. More of a mini-kidnapping and interrogation."

The reception at the Martha Washington is a real shopping bag of Luis' friends and restaurant customers. Eclectic doesn't cover this crowd. Reminds me of Branchtown's multi-cultural, four-generational Night Court. Except for the lack of concealed knives and belt-mounted pistols.

"You must tell me," Umberto says. "Did this man Santo Vargas appear first as a crow? It is said he travels inside the spirit of animals."

"Ridiculous. But Luis told me not to talk about him."

Umberto hisses.

I shift forward, keeping in line. Mr. Vic's mother is headed over here, working her way steadily through the crowd. Mama Bones Bonacelli is not what she seems, that is an old school, Italian grandmother-slash-widow, all in black. This granny has crime connections and paranormal hobbies. I know she eats dinner at Luis' once in a while—often on Friday's for Umberto's Veracruz fish stew—but it surprises me she's at the reception. I didn't see her at the ceremony.

Umberto presses closer. "I will ask what happened of Luis," he says. "*You*...you are a fornicator of sheep."

"Sorry."

Mama Bones bumps into one drink and spills another in her hurried effort to reach me. In a word, she's eager. I hope not to attack me. She's some kind of underboss in Branchtown's illegal, boardwalk-based gambling operation, and though we used to be friendly, she hasn't spoken to me much since I took control of Shore Securities several months ago. Her son Vic founded the place. Hired me as a rookie. Now he has to tolerate me as his boss. Wouldn't surprise me if Vic asked his mother to have me killed.

"'Allo, Austin," Mama Bones says. "You look very handsome today in your tuxedo."

Handsome? "Thanks. You're looking pretty good yourself."

My comment is nervous and bad flattery I hope the old lady ignores. Mama Bones is wearing what she always wears—a simple, high-neck, ankle-length black dress. She's worn only long, black dresses since her husband died in 1994.

"You big sweetie," she says.

My blood pressure jumps as Mama Bones clicks open her black leather purse. The bag is big enough to hold an Uzi, and I'm wondering if planned assassination is behind her surprising friendliness. Bobby G teases me all the time about Mama Bones putting out a contract on me, but I figure enough time has passed since I took over Shore. If she was going to get violent, she would have done so by now.

Besides, like I told Rags, deep down she loves me.

Mama Bone's wrinkled hand reappears from inside her purse with a one ounce perfume bottle. I watch fascinated as she removes the top, flips the glass container, wetting her finger with the little bottle's contents. Next she slowly rubs the stuff behind each of her bulldog ears.

"It's a brand new scent," Mama Bones says. "Straight from Paris." She leans closer to me. "Go on, take a whiff, you handsome devil."

To humor her, I bend down to take an exaggerated inhalation near her perfumed neck. *Whoa.* The ceiling spins. The floor opens. I sense myself falling into an abyss. Rotten citrus, spoiled meat, and the discharge from a construction-site portable potty. Yikes, what an odor. Paris, huh? Smells more like the black hole of Calcutta.

"You like it?" Mama Bones says.

Gasping for air, I try not to make a face, but I can't help myself. "A bit strong for my tastes." I cough. "But it's definitely...uh, unique."

Mama Bones cackles like a chicken, pushes me forward. "Better get your smooch," she says. She ushers me toward the top of the reception line. Solana, the new Mrs. Luis Guerrero, is kissing the man in front of me—Umberto. That means I'm next and that I almost missed my turn by sniffing Mama Bone's ghastly perfume. I still might pass out. Where did she get that stuff?

Oh my, time to forget Mama Bones. Luis' new wife is one of the most ferociously beautiful women I've ever been this close to. Black shiny hair, skin like the creamy latte. I'd use more sexual innuendo to describe her body, her spirit, her overall attractiveness, but this is *Luis'* wife.

I shift my weight to step into Solana's arms, but a strong hand spins me away. Before I even recognize who has me, Patricia Willis presses her drunken mouth against mine. It's a very friendly wine-flavored kiss, let me say, not something repulsive. In fact, it's very sexy—wet and wild, greasy even with the bright red lipstick. But then Patricia pulls away mumbling words about "winning the lottery."

Why talk? Who cares what she *says*? What a kiss that woman just laid on me. Spicy. Stunning. I feel odd, hot. Lost. The taste of her stings my lips like chili oil. She grins at me.

My gaze dives into hers, those blue sky eyes. A buzzing jingles in my ears. "Did you say something?" I say.

"We're going to be rich," Patricia whispers. "My brother says the merger will be announced Monday."

Huh? I sort of want to ask, what does she mean, *we*, but I can't make a sound. My lips, my jaw and my throat are fluttering like wind chimes. Jeez, that was some kiss.

Magical.

I'm dreaming of Patricia's kiss when the sound of a hotel-room key card sliding into the lock snaps me awake. My left hand extends into blackness for the bedside lamp, the brass switch chilly on my fingertips. Then I change my mind. Let's keep room 233 at The Martha Washington dark.

This was not supposed to happen.

Beneath my pillow, I locate and grip the old semiautomatic Colt .45 Umberto loaned me. Having enlisted several of Luis' friends to post guard, stand watch, and otherwise protect my baited butt, I figured the room I gave Santo Vargas would be the safest bet of all Branchtown hiding spots. The gun is with me because I once made the same *safe bet* comment about General Motors bonds one month before bankruptcy.

The room door pushes open until restrained by an old fashioned brass chain. A dark silhouette flashes past a thin shaft of light from the hallway. Santo Vargas? How could he get through all those hombre pals of Luis? Maybe it's not Vargas. Or maybe my guards went home. The clock does read six minutes after four o'clock.

"It is *you* in there, is it not?" Vargas says. "The stockbroker? I can smell you."

Vargas' growl vibrates the bruised flesh on my forehead—as if the broken skin recognized its tormentor. My breathing notches higher.

"Why do you not speak?" he whispers. "Be proud that you have tricked me into coming here without good reason."

I roll off the bed, lift the Colt with both hands, arms extended toward the doorway and Santo Vargas like the cops taught me on *Law and Order* and the other police shows I loved to watch when I was married. Music drifts down the hotel hallway like drizzling rain. More jazz, I think. From the upstairs bar. Piano with a gloomy bass line.

"Proud of tricking you?" I say. "I have more trouble hitting the toilet when I pee."

The weight of Umberto's Colt tugs on my arms.

"You are a funny man," Vargas says. "And a skilled liar. I believed you had betrayed your friend Luis."

"Must be my training in professional sales."

My nose tastes the harsh odor of petrochemicals—a solvent discharging from my borrowed weapon, I suppose. Vargas' silhouette shifts briefly in the doorway.

"Solana has left on her honeymoon?" he says.

I should call nine-one-one. Or shoot this son-of-a-bitch. But no. I feel like chatting. Maybe I have a death wish. What's that liquid sound?

"That's right," I say. "She and Luis are off for the mountains of Tibet. You can beat them there if you fly nonstop."

It's true Luis and his new bride should be cruising high above the Atlantic about now, but not to Tibet. They're going somewhere I don't know. Better safe than sorry, Luis and I both figured.

What is he putting on the floor? I can't see much in the single shaft of light.

"Unfortunately I have other business here," Vargas says. "But before I leave next week, I may still cut out your eyeballs. I do not like liars."

My chin points high. The weapon in my hands gives me confidence. "Get in line, turkey."

Vargas' hand extends through the opened doorway. He lights a match or a plastic lighter. A fist-sized fire erupts around the match, then falls to the floor...*whoosh.* Six-foot flames engulf the doorway and blow even higher to the ceiling. The flash of summer sun and fiery heat knock me backward. The hotel carpet between myself and Vargas explodes in flames. The whole room is on fire.

I fire the semiautomatic toward a doorway I no longer see. Flames block my vision, warm my face and suppress the sound of the old Colt 1911. A red light blinks. An electronic alarm screeches. Water sputters, then sprays from four fixtures in the ceiling. The high-pitched jagged squeal of a fire alarm pierces through the snapping flames. For two or ten seconds—it's hard to judge time—I'm confused what to do. The room is on fire. I have to get out. But the only exits—the door and the window—appear blocked. The still-chained doorway has become a wall of flames. My second-floor glass window to the parking lot is double-thick and sealed shut. I tried getting fresh air earlier.

The answer is in my hand. This time the blasts from Umberto's weapon reassure me. I aim two shots at the sealed glass, one high left, one low right, and the glass explodes. The flames surge behind me, sucked toward my back by the broken window. I grab my trousers off the chair, wrap them around my forearm, use the padded club to clean off the remaining window glass.

I lower myself down to within six feet of the hotel's landscaping, drop and roll.

Unhurt, I stay quiet for a few seconds, pull on my pants with my wallet and cell phone inside, then race away in the shadows. I've survived two confrontations with Vargas now. I do not like the odds on a third.

Fifteen minutes and five blocks later, I'm tired of skulking. I take a cab to the police station and report the fire and the shooting. I left Umberto's Colt in the hotel room beside the window—the room registered to me. I see no way out of telling the truth, or why I'd be in serious trouble if I do. All the Branchtown Police Department's bald, fifty-year-old desk sergeant wants to know is why I didn't hang around the hotel, talk to the detectives who left ten minutes ago for the scene. I even tell the cops about Vargas.

SIX

With the New York Stock Exchange opening bell only minutes away, I'm at home with my laptop Monday morning, logging onto Carr Securities' official website. The fire and my confrontation with Vargas, even the questioning by fire and police officials all day Sunday—yesterday—it's all a nasty dream. What's on my mind now is Patricia, that wet kiss we shared and her prediction the merger would be announced today.

And oh my, *something* is happening. On the live stock screen, Fishman Corp. has an asterisk by its symbol. Extended-hour trading in the company's stock was halted fifty minutes ago. I click on the call letters for Fishman, scroll down and find the latest news headline, the hot flash now spreading across Wall Street and the world: GENE-PAK TO ACQUIRE FISHMAN FOR $46 A SHARE.

My jaw falls. If I'd bought those call options Mr. Greedy considered, Patricia's inside scoop would have netted me and my kids three hundred, maybe three hundred and fifty thousand dollars—depending on where the stock price opens and the options trade. The forty-six dollar price tag is bigger than anyone could have expected.

I sigh and tell myself I did the right thing.

Parking behind Carr Securities around eleven o'clock, I stride through operations and down the center corridor of our big sales room. The whole place stares at me. Every freaking salesman. The only explanation is Bobby G spread the news that Fishman was on my screen last week—the same Fishman now trading twelve dollars higher than it did Friday.

I need shelter. Quick, before they see my face. I didn't make any money on Patricia's inside information, but I knew, and can imagine how guilty I must look. Even Mr. Vic's office seems like refuge.

As usual, Mr. Vic is hard at work. His plain-tipped black shoes rest on top of his desk. He's reading the Branchtown paper. The television's on, Fox Business News showing a variety of talking heads above a live stock market feed with current prices.

I close Vic's office door so we're alone. "I didn't get a chance to ask you at the wedding. Did you and Patricia Willis buy Fishman stock?"

Mr. Vic's attention remains on the local sports section, as if the Rumson Bulldogs' latest victory on the football field held greater news value than the insider trading scam we might be mixed up in. Five beats later, he flips a page, says, "Yeah, I noticed you were busy at Luis' wedding...mainly kissing my girlfriend."

"Your drunk girlfriend kissed *me.* Out of excitement. She said her brother claimed the merger was going through today."

Mr. Vic switches from sports news to financial. So nonchalant. My junior partner is the absolute King of Bull. It makes him a great salesman, but a bad business associate.

"So did you buy Fishman or not?" I say. "As an officer of Carr Securities, you have an obligation—"

Mr. Vic looks at me over the paper. "It would be a lot better if we don't discuss Fishman Corp. or Patricia Willis. Not until we're sure there won't be legal problems."

"Legal problems?"

"Let's wait and see if the SEC or the exchanges announce an investigation."

"You're telling me you and Patricia *did* buy Fishman stock?"

"I'm telling you we shouldn't discuss it," Vic says. "Two weeks or two months from now, some federal prosecutor could ask you or me what we said to each other today. Lying in that situation could put you in jail, right?"

I nod. "No lying to the feds, that's a law."

"But by then maybe you telling the truth could put me or Patricia in jail."

"Oh shit, Vic. You didn't?"

"So let's not discuss it," he says.

I'm not sure I'm verbal anyway. I can't believe Mr. Vic—my mentor and former boss—I can't *believe* he would involve himself in a crime. Or at least illegal activity where his involvement could be so easily proved.

"Anything else?" Mr. Vic says.

Mama Bones stares at her lifetime supply of virgin olive oil—forty-eight, two-gallon corked jars stacked on a pallet in the corner of her basement kitchen. If she poured out all the jars into a tub, there's probably enough greenish liquid to boil that redhead alive.

But how could she heat up the tub?

She walks over by the basement door where she can see the stairway. "Hey, Gianni," she says. "Come down here a minute, huh?"

Mama Bones worries what to tell her son Vic. She could use some help.

When dark haired Gianni scrambles down the stairs and pokes his head inside her basement kitchen, she motions to the round table with a bottle of Paisano and glasses in the center. Her nephew has on blue jeans and a white T-shirt. Must be warm outside.

"You wanna glass of wine?" she says.

"No, Mama Bones, I'm kind of busy. You need something?"

She coughs.

"What's the matter?" Gianni says.

"Vic is gonna be mad."

"Something happen at the wedding? You looked pissed off when you got home."

"You know Vic's redheaded *comare*?"

"Patty?" Gianni says. "Patty Willis?"

"She calls herself Patricia now."

"Fancy." Gianni glances over his shoulder, showing her he wants to leave.

"So just-a when Austin Carr is about to kiss the bride at the wedding, right when he's going to fall in love with his best friend's brand new wife, that Patricia Willis comes along and ruins everything. *She* kisses Austin, notta the bride."

"I don't get it," Gianni says.

Mama Bones makes a choking noise. "Listen. I make a love potion. I get Austin Carr to sniff it. Now he's gonna fall in love with the next person he kisses. That's the magic of the potion, and I give it to him right when he's next in line to kiss the bride at Luis' wedding. Her name is Solana, I think."

Gianni laughs. "Okay. Now I get it. That's the potion you made the other day?"

"Right. So instead of Luis' new wife, now Austin Carr is in love with my son Vic's *comare*."

Gianni snorts, holding back laughter.

Mama Bones hisses at him. "What should I say, huh? He's gonna be real mad, right?"

Gianni shakes his head. He's grinning ear to ear. "Don't worry about it. Vic won't believe a word. He's going to want his twenty thousand, though."

"You heard about the bet?"

When Gianni nods, she pushes him out of the basement, closes the heavy steel door on his face. The son of a gun. Gianni doesn't believe one word about Aunt Maria's magic love spell. He thinks this is all a big joke.

She grabs the cell phone from her purse. Better to get it over.

"'Allo, Vic?"

"I'm really busy, Mama. I have two clients on hold."

"Okay, you wanna be like that, it's fine. It's only your poor old mama on the phone. No reason for you to listen or take a little time to talk."

"Ditch the accent, will you?"

"You're a badda-bad boy, Vittorio."

"Tell me what you want."

Mama Bones shakes her head, her gaze on the olive oil jars. This is how Vic makes her feel all the time. Like something stored away. "Listen, so you know—I made Austin Carr fall in love with your girlfriend Patricia."

Silence.

She imagines Vic shaking his head on the other end of the telephone, like maybe his Mama is a fool. He makes her mad sometimes. "You remember Austin Carr, right? He's the guy who took control of your business?"

Vic sighs so loud, he sounds like the wind.

"You can't make someone fall in love," Vic says. "You can't make Patricia do *anything*. Believe me."

"Aunt Maria's love potion is very famous in *Napoli*. It's-a how I catch your father Domenic."

"Ah, Ma."

"What, huh?"

Silence, then Vic says, "So are you going to pay up the twenty thousand you owe me?"

With her right hand, Mama Bones chokes her telephone. "You owe *me*, smarty pants. Aunt Maria's potion worked perfect. Austin Carr took one sniff and turned into a drooling dog over your girlfriend when she smooched him. The stuff is so strong, she fell for him, too."

"Fine. That's what you called to tell me? You're welching on the bet and my girlfriend's fallen in love with Austin Carr. Is that really why you called me, Ma? Thanks a bunch."

Mama Bones bites a knuckle so hard, there's blood when she stops.

SEVEN

I'm on a trading desk telephone a few days later, checking bond quotes and talking with a client when Bobby G slips alongside me. "Look at your news ticker," he says. "Fishman."

I tell a client to hold on, pinch the telephone between my ear and shoulder, then type in Fishman's call letters. Immediately I see what Bobby G's talking about: *Stock Price Rise Before Merger Prompts Insider Investigation of Fishman.*

My stomach suicides off a fourteen-story building. The U.S. Securities and Exchange Commission and the U.S. District Attorney for New York have agreed to jointly investigate "unusual option and stock trading" prior to the Fishman, Gene-Pak merger announcement. It appears as "person or persons unknown maybe profited from prior knowledge" of the pending merger announcement.

Oh, hell, Mr. Vic. I hope you haven't done anything *extraordinarily* stupid.

I jump up and check Vic's office. He's not there.

On the way back to my desk, I try his cell phone and then his home. No Vic. I stop by Carmela's seat on the trading desk.

"He was here a few minutes ago," Vic's daughter says. "I'm sure he'll be right back."

After a Mexican dinner at Luis', most of the time spent contemplating the loss of my stockbroker's license, prison or worse, like maybe selling used Fiats, I stalk home to my condo, preparing to turn on the television and sulk.

Vic's my junior partner, President of Carr Securities, and he still hasn't returned my calls. I can't find him. I'm completely in the dark about what he has or hasn't done about that Fishman tip, and I am so absorbed with potential disaster, I fail to notice the extra-large dead animal on my doorstep until I nearly trip over it.

What the heck *is* that? Looks like a pile of skinned rabbits. Oh, *hell* no.

It's my teenage daughter Beth, hiding beneath what is undoubtedly her mother's finest winter fur coat. My heart jumps against my ribcage. Is she hurt? I touch her shoulder. Beth's breathing is solid and rhythmic. Her color is pink, and her cheek warms the back of my fingers. She's sleeping.

"Beth, wake up. Are you okay?"

My sixteen-year-old lifts her head. Her blue eyes droop with sleepiness. Beth's blond hair used to be long and clean, but now it's football-helmet short, and dyed midnight. Her eyes and lips are also painted black—like a Goth rock star. I taste a whiff of beer in the air.

Her eyes focus slowly. "Daddy?"

"What happened to hoodies and the ponytail?" I say.

She staggers to her feet and gives me a hug. At least some things haven't changed.

"I'm sixteen now," she says.

In the porch light, a sparkle blinks at me from her nose. A piercing? What the heck is going on with Miss Goody Two Shoes, the straight-A student? From sophomore class vice president to Queen Glitter Rock in a week?

"I thought you went to Hilton Head with your mom and Bob," I say.

"They're leaving tomorrow, but I'm not going. I need a break from Mother, not Jersey."

I can relate. In fact, that line would make a good slogan for the entire state, except not everyone's Mom or ex-wife is Susan the Succubus. I slip my key into my condo's lock.

Beth has her own bedroom here anyway, although when she and Ryan aren't visiting, I use the desk in her room as my home office. I put fresh towels in the smaller bath and clean sheets on her bed, then write down my new password for the desktop. When she's busy on my computer, allegedly doing homework, I call Beth's mother. Bob the Dentist answers with a distinctly pissed off tone.

"Sorry to bother you," I say, "but I need to talk to Susan. It's important."

"I will not bother Susan," Bob says. "She has not been well."

Susan hasn't been well since 2005. "It's about Beth," I say.

"I do not care what it's about," Bob says. "You can tell Susan in the morning. Before we go to Hilton Head."

Bob is such a dope. A few years ago I might have gotten angry, driven over there and chased him around the house. But you have to be jealous to get that kind of angry, and I'm not jealous anymore. Like lust, anger and the soft flesh of youth, everything I ever felt for Susan has faded with time.

"Fine," I say. "When Susan's looking for her daughter tomorrow, tell her to call me."

"What? Okay, okay, wait." I hear a bang, like the phone hitting a table. But there's no dial tone, so I hang on. Thirty seconds later, Susan's buzz-saw voice shows up.

"Is Beth with you?" Susan says.

"Yes. I found her on my doorstep when I came home tonight."

"Is she hurt?"

"She's fine. Doing her homework."

"Are you going to bring her home?"

I take a breath. "She wants to stay here tonight."

"We're going to Hilton Head tomorrow right after school. She has to pack."

"I'll bring her over in the morning. Before school."

It's two or three beats before Susan says, "She complained about me, didn't she? She called me a bitch right to my face yesterday."

"She's a teenager," I say.

"Oh, aren't we understanding. I suppose you agreed with her?"

"Actually, I didn't. I told her how—"

"You know what, Austin. Why don't you just keep that little snot for the rest of her miserable life."

Whoa. "Little snot?"

"I don't believe I have one working gene in that screwed up pool of hers."

"Beth needs a family atmosphere," I say. "She should be with you, her brother. Not with her single father."

"I'm serious, Austin. You're so understanding of her condition, you take her for a while."

"But I—"

The line goes dead.

The next morning at seven, I knock on Beth's bedroom door.

"Wake up, honey. Time to get up."

Silence.

"I talked to your mother last night. You don't have to go to Hilton Head. But I thought you might want to go by your house this morning and pick up fresh clothes before school."

Nothing. Her room is dead quiet, even with my ear pressed to the door.

"Beth?"

I knock again, then try the door. Locked.

I'm done talking to wood. I lope through my condo, out the front door, then down through the narrow garden of palm trees and elephant-ear philodendrons along the west side of my building. Crows squawk and fight over something in the neighbor's privet hedge.

Near the back of my ground-floor two-bedroom, a redwood stake fence curtains off every condo's small but private patio—more like horse stalls, each with its own garden gate. The areas are good for barbecuing. Mine is located outside my office, or Beth's room. I open my gate and see the sliding glass door to Beth's room is wide open. I run inside the room and spot a handwritten note on a stack of her school books.

Daddy. Got a ride to school. See you tonight.

My heart rate slows, but not all the way. She went to school without her Math, English, or Science books and a notebook of homework assignments.

There's writing on the back of the notebook. A few doodles, some phone numbers, and what looks like two lines of free verse.

Kneel before the devil
She has accessed your soul

Nice. Beth's writing satanic poetry. Probably about her mother Susan.

I take comfort in my routine of shower, dress, and the short drive to work, but my head reels with new responsibilities and the certain knowledge that familiar pastimes are marked for change. A teenage daughter is one thing. A live-in teenage daughter is quite another.

Instinct tells me Beth needs my under-appreciated parenting skills, but instinct also tells me it's an assignment fraught with trouble. I feel like a middle-aged Army reservist being called up to the front lines in Afghanistan.

At my desk, first thing to do is call Beth's school. After an odd exchange, in which I'm forced to reveal my Social Security number, driver's license, my mother's maiden name and the variety of my ex-wife's sexual appetites, I discover my daughter indeed arrived safely at school. And on time, too.

Good. I can put aside my worries for the next half-dozen hours and concentrate on earning a living.

Wrong. Patricia Willis ruins work shortly after ten o'clock. I know my day is over as soon as I hear her voice, too, because in my mind, the noisy salesroom goes dead silent and the light in the big room shifts brighter: Like after that second stiff martini, the world has been altered, and the next few hours can only hold adventure.

"Meet me at the beach for lunch," she says. "I think we have something to talk about."

"Like you being Vic's girlfriend?" I say.

"Like that kiss."

I pull the receiver away from my ear and stare at the plastic. Did she feel something special when our lips touched—like me? My office telephone looks like it always did. Black. Oblong. Little holes for the Austin Carr Gift of Gab to flow through. But nothing else seems the same. The air is moving strangely. I need to talk to Patricia.

The phone gets back against my ear in time to hear the redhead say, "One-thirty at Clooney's. I'll meet you at the outside beach bar."

EIGHT

The strip of Branchtown Municipal Beach directly in front of Clooney's restaurant consists of crushed rock and broken white shells, a crunchy, gritty bleached soup of stone and dead sea creatures. Pelicans cruise above the rolling surf, a low, single-file line flying south. I am so excited to be with Patricia I can hardly breathe. We've been walking without speaking for ten minutes when she accidentally-on-purpose bumps my hip with her own.

"What would you say happened when we kissed at Luis' wedding?" Patricia says. She's wearing tan shorts and a black sweater rising and falling like the ocean when she breathes. She obviously didn't come here from a job. "What did you *feel*?"

"I'm not sure," I say. "An odd kind of heat on my lips."

She stares at me. "Sex you mean?"

"No. More like chili peppers."

She laughs. "I like the sound of that."

Her earthy giggle makes me want to grab her. Her voice is like a magnet. "And I've dreamed about you every night since."

Patricia touches my arm and we stop walking. A wave crashes on our left and washes against our bare feet. The ocean water freezes my toes. Patricia's fingers heat my skin. I reach and gently turn her shoulder. We kiss.

Consuming fire breaks out wherever our bodies touch. There are more kisses, an agonizing two-minute sensation of burning alive, awkward words about my car, her coming in a taxi, and where. We haven't been together thirty minutes before we're driving to my place, trying not to touch each other in the Camry. It's impossible.

As soon as my condo door snaps closed behind us, Patricia clutches for me, her hands and arms demanding, circling my waist like boa constrictors. Her body presses against me, melting into me, soft and entrapping. When she lifts her face toward mine, parting her lips, I worry I will be devoured. The passion I feel is unknown to me, the electric silk touch of her skin like nothing I've ever experienced.

The rapping at my front door is polite, not urgent or rude, but highly intrusive, although I'm not going to describe exactly what I'm doing. In my quickly donned boxer shorts, I crack open the front door of my condo and greet a man and woman in their mid-thirties, neither one much to look at, but both stylishly dressed and clean-cut. Smart looking. New York, I'm guessing.

Both of them hold up badges and New York U.S. District Attorney identification cards. Jeez. It's the Feds from Manhattan after a poor Jersey boy.

The man says, "Austin Carr?"

"Yes."

"We're with the U.S. District Attorney's Office for New York. We'd like to talk to you about your purchase of Fishman Corp. stock options."

My face hardens into a package of frozen peas. Wind plays with the yellow-leafed maples behind my front-porch guests and brings a buzz of traffic from the nearby intersection. Whatever romantic sensations had been flowing through me—body, heart and soul—are now blown away or shrunken. There's a taste of auto exhaust and federal prison on the breeze.

"I thought you were Jehovah's Witnesses," Patricia says.

Whoa. Patricia scares me, sneaking up behind. She's wearing the couch blanket draped over her shoulder like a Roman senator.

The female agent says, "May we come in and talk?"

My heart thuds, the rhythm double-timing the tick-tock of my living room clock. My palms ooze like a crushed carton of eggs. *My purchase of Fishman Corp. stock options.* I can only manage a half-boat Carr grin. "There's been a mistake of some sort. I didn't buy Fishman options."

"Nothing official yet, Mr. Carr, but lying to us later will be a crime," the woman says. Her hair is dull brown, the pageboy too short for her ears. Her thick lobes look like double-wheels on a truck. "We've already subpoenaed and examined your accounts. The record shows you bought Fishman call options three days before the announcement and sold the day of the news. You turned fifty thousand dollars into more than three hundred thousand."

I'm shaking my head in protest when everything hits. The truth shines. The light goes on. The bell rings. The poop hits the fan: Mr. Vic inviting me to hear Patricia's story; him refusing to discuss the merger after it was announced; and the clincher, Vic knowing I rarely trade or check my personal account.

"Let us come in and talk about it, Mr. Carr," the young man says. "I really need to use the restroom."

I shake my head. "No. Wait here."

Turning my back on the Feds, leaving Patricia to keep them outside, I check my laptop on the kitchen counter. The ticking of my mantle clock becomes the soundtrack of a Hitchcock thriller, a menacing echo when I see my account. Crap. The U.S. Attorney's Office has my butt, all right. Austin Carr's net worth has jumped by three hundred and fifteen grand. The cash is located in my money-market fund now, but by clicking HISTORY, I see the Fed's version of my alleged Fishman option trading is indeed the accurate record.

Vic must have used his partner's master account code to trade in my account, set me up. He sold my mutual funds I have for the kids, put everything in Fishman options.

I check Patricia. From my new angle at the kitchen counter, I notice her makeshift toga doesn't hide her entire left buttocks. Well, at least she's got the *federales* covered. My fingers fumble inside my wallet for something I need desperately. There.

Striding back to my would-be interrogators, I hand the woman a business card. "I'd rather not speak to you without my attorney present," I say. "I'm sure he'll be happy to set up an appointment for us all to talk."

The young woman stares at the slick business card of Randall Zimmer III, my highly competent attorney. Her partner leans over to read it as well.

"You've already hired a lawyer in this matter?" he says.

"I'm a *Jersey* stockbroker, pal. I keep one on retainer."

Shaking her head, Mama Bones lets the binoculars hang loose, the straps resting on her bosom. She reaches into her black purse for her cell phone. She had no idea Austin Carr was so kinky. Imagine. Inviting another man and woman to his condo for group sex.

"Hey, Vic," Mama Bones says. "Guess where your *comare* spent the last hour, huh?"

"Tell me you are not watching Patricia."

"Sure I am. Why not? But guess where she is. Patricia, who you say I can't make do anything. Come on. Guess where she is now? No? Okay, I tell you. She's answering Austin's doorbell without any clothes on."

"You're saying she's with Carr?"

"That's right. Austin Carr. He not only takes your business. Now he takes your *comare,* too. Hope you don't have nothing else he wants."

"Ma. Please. If you're telling me the truth, the news is hurtful. If you're lying, it's even worse. Why would you do this?"

"I'm sorry. I can't help telling you Patricia and Austin Carr spent the last hour playing hide the salami in his condo."

"Ma."

"Sometimes my magic works," she says. "Now maybe you listen to me once in a while when I call. Give me the time of day."

"How about I come for dinner tonight?"

"That's nice. I'll make your favorite—the white clam sauce. And bring the twenty thousand, okay?"

NINE

Not long after the sun goes down and my condo turns dark, Patricia Willis whispers it's time for her to leave. She says her cat needs food and milk, asks can she have a ride home. We've spent all afternoon in bed but I still don't want her to go.

Inside my Camry, the smell of her keeps me wanting.

She says, "Please believe I had nothing to do with the tampering in your investment account. I ended up giving my brother money to invest for me, gave him your advice on Panama. I told Vic he was on his own."

"I believe you," I say. "It had to be Vic put money in my account. He and the back office are the only people with access, and only Vic would know to buy Fishman call options. He's the only one heard your story, right?"

"Right."

"So you gave him an idea, that's all. He's trying to set me up for insider trading, get my securities license taken away."

"Here we are," Patricia says. "Second driveway on the right. And thank you for bringing me home. I'm sorry to move the...uh, festivities, but my cat will tear the couch up if I don't come home and feed her. Besides, after those District Attorney people showed up, your place lost a touch of its romance."

I grin at her. "I didn't notice."

She gently slaps my shoulder, then squeezes my leg.

Under the weight of her hand, the skin on my thigh tingles. Her happy voice is like a time machine, throwing my mind back to our first love-making on my couch. I can still picture the freckles on her white breasts, hear the throaty pleasure in her laughter.

I'm stupid crazy about her. It's like Cupid shot me in the heart. I don't even mind Vic pointed me toward jail on insider trading charges. I'll worry about my problems later—

outsmarting Vic hasn't been difficult so far. Patricia is everything right now. The excitement I feel—well, it's more than another new redhead in my life. Truthfully, I have never been so strongly attracted to anyone.

Maybe I've been zapped by the love mojo.

Patricia points because I'm about to miss the second driveway. I swing the Camry into a dark lane between four-story trees, the gravel road extending one hundred yards into a miniature forest of evergreens and undergrowth, well out of sight of the road. Man-high ferns and rhododendrons grow beneath the trees. Fading yellow hostas form a close border on both sides of the gravel. Their dead flower stalks mark the road like a snow fence.

At the end of the driveway my headlights illuminate a Victorian carriage house, the structure built—I'm guessing—for servants of the century old mansion standing next door. The main place is as big as a hotel. Though Patricia's rental unit is one-sixth the size, the two buildings share a maroon and white color combination, matching shake roofs, the same scrolling window trim, and a substantial dock on the Navasquan River.

"Come on in and meet my cat," she says.

The world turns nearly black when my headlights fade. The main house lies to the right, behind a collection of blue and green conifers, and I can't see the roof line anymore. The steady putt-putt of a small outboard engine buzzes on the river. Looking for the sound I see flickering lights on the water.

I follow Patricia up an exposed wooden stairway on the right side of her carriage house. A new Jaguar two-seater and a Mercedes 310 fill the garage spaces below her apartment. The stairway creaks as Patricia rises ahead of me to the second floor. My gaze follows her hips.

"Let's get naked as soon as you feed the cat," I say. "I have to pick up Beth at the library in an hour."

Patricia laughs. "How about a drink first, sweet talker. I'm thirsty."

Rusty hinges squeak as she keys open her front door. The paint on the staircase flakes off under my touch.

I follow Patricia inside the dark front room, watch her flip on the light switch. A seascape hangs on the opposite wall. Over her shoulder, a faded green sofa is half covered with newspapers and magazines.

Patricia shrieks.

I don't see why, or what's on the other half of the green sofa until I jump all the way inside to protect her. Mr. Vic Bonacelli sits calmly on the sofa. He's holding a pistol.

Vic stares at me with scary wide eyes.

"What's up with the gun?" I say. "And why did you fill up my personal investment account with Fishman options?"

Vic is normally an affable guy. He loves to play golf and tell jokes. Maybe that's what this semiautomatic pistol is, a joke. I'm sure hoping.

"Two reasons I'm showing you the gun," Vic says. "One, I need to talk to Patricia alone, and I don't want to waste time arguing with you."

I nod. Seems reasonable to me. I said he was affable. Heck, so I am.

"Two," Vic says, "I don't want you to speak to Patricia ever again, and I figured this Glock nine-millimeter would help you understand the depth of my feelings."

I glance at Patricia. Her gaze flits low to her extreme left, the movement so rapidly connected to my gaze, the action seems a signal. My gaze follows hers to an aluminum briefcase on the floor, tucked in the far north corner of the room. "Sure, Vic, whatever you say. What about the Fishman options in my account. You set me up so I'd lose my license? Be forced to sell out the business to you?"

"That's exactly what I have in mind," Vic says. "Patricia handed me a perfect opportunity. I couldn't resist."

I must say, I'm a bit shocked Mr. Vic harbors such venom. Maybe I shouldn't have changed the name of our firm to Carr Securities. The Glock in his hand looks more menacing than it did ten seconds ago: I'm beginning to understand Vic might be angry enough to shoot me.

I take a light hold of Patricia's arm. "Maybe we should go."

She shakes her head. "I need to talk to him, Austin. You go. I'll call you later."

I want to do whatever those sky blue eyes ask, so I look away. "He's got a loaded gun pointed at us. I am *not* leaving you here."

"The gun is for you," Vic says. "I've got something else for Patricia."

Steam boils my neck, but Patricia's on me fast, embracing me, pushing her pretty face close to mine, leaning her weight so we stagger backward to the open doorway.

"Go pick up your daughter," she whispers. "Let me handle Vic. He's not going to hurt me. It's about that briefcase."

"I've known Vic a long time," I say. "But tonight he looks like a guy I don't know—dangerous."

Vic hears me and grins.

"He's jealous, that's all," she whispers. "Now go, or there *will* be trouble. Let me handle him. You have to trust me."

"I don't want to leave you."

"Please. Trust me."

Vic stands and tucks the Glock behind his back. "I would never hurt Patricia. I don't want to shoot you either, Austin. But I will if I ever see you with her again."

"Go," she says.

An hour later, waiting in the car for my daughter Beth, my brain exercises. One subject: I had no idea Mr. Vic was so attached to the redhead he'd pull a gun on me, threaten my life. The man is married thirty years, has several girlfriends. What am I missing? Second subject: Patricia failed to inform me of a few things as well, like what was in that briefcase and why would she point it out to me. Having fallen quickly and hard for Mr. Vic's redhead, I'm also a little worried what Patricia and Vic are doing right now in her apartment.

Another woman startles me out of jealous concern—my daughter leans inside the Camry's open passenger window wearing enough purple lipstick and eye-shadow to star in a 1920 silent movie.

"Hi, Daddy. Is it okay if Mike takes me home?"

I catch my breath. I had been imagining Patricia in such detail, Beth scared me. Gusts of cold wind make a mess of the Branchtown Public Library's two acres of landscaped park. Oak trees throw leaves on the front sidewalk. I need to stop worrying about Patricia, consider my responsibilities.

"Daddy?"

"Who's Mike?" I say.

Beth frowns. "I told you this afternoon. Mike Branigan. His family lives on our street. We've been classmates since fourth grade."

He sounds vaguely familiar.

"Daddy, you sell his mother and father tax-free bonds."

Now I remember. I've watched Mike grow up. I must still be thinking about Patricia's freckles. "Okay, but Mike's bringing you straight home, right? No parties or movies or trips to the mall. It's a school night."

"We'll be right behind you," she says.

Driving away, my heart takes funny turns. Beth's of my own flesh, a part of me, and now she's begun to pull away, testing herself against the world. A child becoming a woman. I have to find a way to spend more time with her, and Ryan, too.

Soon as I get home and make coffee, my forehead starts to sweat. Ten minutes pass with me watching the clock. What was I *thinking?* Why did I say yes to Mike Branigan bringing my daughter home?

Fifteen minutes go by. I drink a cup of coffee.

Half an hour. I finish the pot.

Finally! My kitchen clock says forty-five minutes have passed when the front door pops open and Beth strolls in, her jaws working on a wad of gum.

"Where were you?" I say.

"I needed something at the drug store," Beth says. "Can I use your desktop to print some homework for school?"

"Sure. But you said you were coming right home. Don't you understand how that worries me?"

"Sorry, Daddy." She scoots into the bathroom and locks the door.

I don't like the way this whole parent-child thing is going. My gut hurts. Beth's off track, I can feel it, and having her for a full-time roommate puts the responsibility squarely on me.

I'm her father. Of course this is on me.

TEN

In her upstairs kitchen, the nice one with a tile floor, windows, flowers and her glassed-in collection of ceramic giraffes, Mama Bones checks the oven clock: Thing says 8:08 in straight and bright blue lines. Her son Vic knew she was making white clam sauce tonight, fettuccini with double-breaded fried veal cutlets. It's not like him to be even a minute late.

Mama Bones calls Gianni. "Is my Vic on his way yet?"

"He's still inside Patricia's place. Or maybe he's just inside Patricia."

"Watch your mouth." Mama Bones bites her knuckle. Did her phone call, her news about Austin and the redheaded slut set Vic off on some tantrum? Her son has a temper for sure, but he couldn't hurt a woman. She taught him better.

"Austin Carr left, right?" she asks.

"Half an hour ago. Like I told you before."

"And Patricia didn't leave, too?" Mama Bones asks. "You sure she's up there with Vic?"

Silence. And Mama Bones doesn't like silence. With Gianni, the quiet means he's thinking hard, trying to figure how to tell her something. She glances at her giraffe collection. They remind her it's good to know what's over the horizon. These long-necked, spotted horse-things can see what's coming.

"Haven't seen Patricia go anywhere," he says.

Something's not quite right with Gianni's words, Mama Bones can tell. He's fudging. "You left?" she says. "Maybe for just a minute?"

Gianni sighs. "Maybe two minutes I was gone," he says. "There's a McDonald's up the street. I needed coffee."

"That's it? You were gone five minutes buying coffee?"

"Yeah."

"No, that's not all, Gianni. There's something else. What?"

He coughs. "Well, when I came back, the Jaguar underneath her apartment was gone, but I'm pretty sure that's not Patricia's car."

"You're *pretty sure?*

"I've never seen her driving it before."

"Go knock on the door," Mama Bones says. "Make sure Vic's in there, that he's okay."

"But he'll know I've been following him."

"Tell him you drove by and saw his car, that you looked for him because his cell phone's off and his mama keeps calling you, asking you to find him, send him here for dinner. Like he promised."

"Okay. Jeez."

It's too quick when Gianni calls back. There was no time for a real conversation between Gianni and Vic, so Mama Bones is afraid something bad has happened to her son. She hesitates answering, finding out what Gianni has to say. Funny, this time it's not so good she can see who is calling. She crosses herself, prays to Mother Mary that her son is alive and well.

Gianni's voice, when he says Mama Bones' name, takes her breath away. She knows his next words will crush her.

"Vic's been shot," Gianni says.

Mama Bones wants to scream like someone sawed off her leg. But instead, her eyes fill with tears, and her throat shrinks so small she can hardly breathe. No screaming for sure. The only sound she can make is a wet gasp.

"I already called nine one one," Gianni says, "and Vic's breathing fine, his heart's beating and everything."

"Oh, Mother Mary!"

"I hear the sirens, Mama Bones. They're almost here. He'll make it."

Mama Bones' chest bone creaks as the pounding heart beneath it swells and prepares to burst. Oh, Mary, Mother of God. Please don't take my Vic.

Take me. Take me, please. This is my fault.

Mama Bones cries all night at the hospital, where her son sleeps in a coma. She cries all day at the church, where she prays. She cries in her bed where she can't sleep. This kind of pain is deep, makes everything taste and smell bad, makes everybody sound like a dope to her when they talk, and makes Mama Bones wish she could be anywhere else but in the room listening to them blab. Even the doctors. They got nothing to say. They don't know.

The days and night run together until at the hospital one night, staring at Vic in his coma, tubes and wires coming out like different thicknesses of spaghetti, Mama Bones remembers why she doesn't like hospitals—her dead husband Domenic. Dom went in for a colonoscopy but woke up with cancer, no colon, a plastic bag attached to his side for poop. When no one was around, he killed himself that first night when he saw, ripping out the wires, draining tubes, IV lines and even the stitches.

Remembering Domenic makes her stop crying because she was so mad at him when he did that. Heck, she's still mad at him for committing that sin. She doesn't understand to this day why he didn't want to live. Sure, pooping into a bag you have to wear is no fun, but Dom still would have had his family. His wife and children. Didn't he love them? Didn't he want his family? They sure loved and needed him.

Just like now. Her family needs her.

Mama Bones stands over the stove frying scrambled eggs in bacon grease for her nephews Gianni and Tomas, members of her crew and permanent residents at her house in Branchtown since her old boss Bluefish was publically assassinated last winter. Gianni loves a big breakfast, but Tomas says he only wants plain white yogurt.

"When did you start eating like a ballerina?" Mama Bones asks.

Tomas grins. Gianni studies her face. His brow is puzzled, wondering maybe why Mama Bones makes a joke when Vic—though getting slightly better—is still in a coma. But Gianni must see the change, her need to start working again. Both nephews know Mama Bones pretty good.

"My friend at Branchtown P.D. says it was Vic's own gun that shot him," Gianni says.

Outside her kitchen window, Mama Bones glimpses three kids on their way to school, laughing, playing kid games. Can it really be thirty-three years since her Vic went off to school down this very street? Laughing like those children. Her wooden spoon pushes around the milk, cheese, and egg mixture so the runny stuff touches heat. Gianni doesn't like his eggs underdone. "It's hard for me to believe Austin Carr took Vic's gun away and shot him," she says. "Needs to be somebody tougher than Austin to do that."

Gianni says, "I'm thinking Patricia shot him. She could have tricked him out of the gun. Got his mind on something else. You know."

Mama Bones sniffs. Gianni says the truth. Vic usually has only one thing on his mind, pretty much all the time. Sex. It's the reason he didn't reach a higher place in this world, and could easily be the reason he got shot—well, sex and his own mother, heating Vic up about his *comare* Patricia. How can Mama Bones not blame herself for this terrible thing?

"So, Gianni," she says. "How you figure this shooting happen, exactly?"

Gianni leans back from the kitchen table. The chair squeaks in terror as his weight spreads on only two legs. "I saw Vic's car parked a block away when I followed Carr and the redhead to her place," he says. "So Vic must have been waiting for them when they walked in. I figure Vic threatened Carr with the gun, told him to stay away from Patricia. But then Carr or the redhead got hold of Vic's gun, shot him with it."

"But you were outside," Tomas says. "Wouldn't you have heard the shot?"

"The house is two hundred yards from the street, behind a forest of thick trees. I might not hear."

"So," Tomas says, "the shooting could have happened either before or after Carr left. Carr could have shot him."

Mama Bones scratches the eggs from her frying pan onto Gianni's plate. "So tell me one thing, Sherlock. Why? Tell me why Vic's *comare* wants to shoot the man she's been sleeping with ten years or more."

Gianni's fork digs into the eggs. "She's fallen for Austin. You saw them at Austin's condo. Maybe Vic wouldn't let her go. It's the oldest 'why' in the world."

Mama Bones does not want to believe such a thing. It can't be true. It would mean that her potion is responsible for Vic's coma. She shakes her head no, says, "Patricia Willis is no murderer. Neither is Austin. I think Vic was up to something behind my back. Something none of us knew about."

"Vic *can* be sneaky," Gianni says, "But I'm not sure he would keep important secrets from you. Stuff that could get him shot."

"I am," she says. "My Vic doesn't need a gun to scare Austin Carr. He had that gun with him for another reason—to protect something valuable."

Mama Bones' nephews glance at each other. Sheepishly, Father Ignacio would say. There is something these two boys haven't told her yet.

"What?" Mama Bones says.

"I mentioned this to Tomas the other day, then forgot," Gianni says. "Vic was carrying a fancy aluminum briefcase the last two days—sturdy, like something a jeweler would use to carry inventory."

ELEVEN

A week after Mr. Vic's shooting, in the offices of Carr Securities, I sign for certified mail, a typed letter with a headline: "SUBPOENA DUCES TECUM." It's from the federal government's Wall Street watchdog, the U. S. Securities and Exchange Commission, and it's addressed to me, Austin Carr.

"You are hereby required to appear before the undersigned and other officers of the Securities and Exchange Commission...to testify in the Matter of Trading in the Securities of Fishman Corp."

The Feds have always been big on capital letters in strange places.

"You are hereby required to bring with you and produce at said time and place those books, papers, documents, and other records described in the Attachment hereto," the letter concludes. "Fail not at your peril."

I call my attorney, Randall Zimmer, Esq. He listens to me rant about how Vic set me up, how Vic hates my guts since I took control of his business, and how only Vic and I have access to the master password. Even to me, my words sound like another litany of excuses from a ne'er do well. Luckily for me, I've got the best mouthpiece in Seaside County, maybe the only German, Irish and Italian weighted Jersey Bar Association allowed in. Mr. Z tells me to stay calm. We set up an appointment to talk and strategize.

Nothing like a subpoena to start the afternoon. I need a strategy session right away. With a bottle. I call to check, get the good news about Luis', inform the receptionist and Carmela, then set out immediately for my favorite hangout. I'm one of thirty customers, Luis standing on the horseshoe bar as I walk inside, Luis hanging a new sombrero he bought in Spain. Much to my happiness, and as I confirmed via telephone, Luis and his bride returned last night from their honeymoon.

A mariachi tune plays over the speaker system. The television is off. Luis' bride Solana is a new waitress, the black hair piled on top of her head, cheeks and lips devoid of the makeup I saw at her wedding. She's prettier this way, really, the lady hustling between tables balancing three enchilada dinner plates, her hips bumping air to the Mexican folk music.

Luis jumps down from the counter to the rubber mat behind his bar. The grace of his leap and soft landing startle me. Smooth and quiet. Luis must be the reincarnation of an ancient Toltec wizard. He dominates his territory like a wild cat.

"So, *mi amigo*," Luis says. "What is it you wish to speak about?"

I don't even ask anymore how he knows I want to talk. There must be something on my face, something directly opposite in meaning to a full-boat grin. I start right in, use maybe three minutes to tell my spiritual advisor about Patricia Willis, about me being at her place before Mr. Vic was shot, and about how Patricia has now disappeared.

"I haven't heard from her since that night," I say.

Luis shrugs. "You must go to the police."

Darn. Why did I ask? I don't want to go to the police, tell them I was there minutes before Vic was shot. When you think about it, who had a better reason to shoot him than me? He tampered with my account, betrayed me.

Better change the subject. "Any sign of that guy Vargas?" I ask.

Luis shakes his head. "No, but I am concerned he will return. That is why I have Solana working here."

I sip my tequila, looking for the right way to phrase my question. Touchy subject I have on my mind. "Is Vargas like...Solana's old boyfriend or something?"

Luis turns his gaze away from me. "Vargas is a story for another day."

Other than minor traffic and the associated vehicle headlights, it's quiet and dark in Luis' parking lot by the time I leave. My shoes kick gravel as I walk between cars, the automobile spaces less than half occupied. My mind considers Patricia and my feelings for her, Mr. Vic's Glock aimed at me, plus the friends my daughter Beth has invited over to watch TV at our place tonight. Consumed with these issues, and thus completely self-absorbed, I don't see the guy in the hoodie until it's way too late. I don't even have time to raise a protective hand.

His fist explodes against my nose and cheek.

I stumble backward, the pain shocking my senses. Everybody's a brawler until they get punched in the face. My hands are up to my face when Hoodie Man kicks me in the crotch. I go down to one knee.

"Where's the cash?" Hoodie Man says.

I have no clue what he's talking about. But I do know this guy is disguising his voice. Maybe I know him. "What cash?"

Luis' parking lot surface consists of one-inch granite gravel, a gray and jagged carpet, and all four million sharp rocks are biting my knee. Under the light of a three-quarter moon, I stop wondering who this bastard is and instead get pissed. This son of a bitch punched and kicked me.

"The cash in the briefcase," he says.

I jump to my feet. Hoodie Man snaps a Chuck Norris front kick into my gut, then pushes me back down. Since all good things come in threes, I roll on my back as soon as I hit the gravel, expecting another foot stomp. He obliges, too, and I'm ready, grabbing his foot and twisting his sneaker like I'm snapping a right turn in the Camry.

He belly flops onto the parking lot gravel with a familiar yelp. I notice the hoodie he wears has a broken zipper. A five inch strip of metal teeth and torn backing dangle from a seam. What briefcase was he talking about—the one Vic brought to Patricia's?

Before I can stand or jump on his back, he sprints away, Hoodie Man's knees nearly touching while he runs. The crazy legs style reminds me of someone, a jerk I saw move like that once down the main aisle of Carr Securities.

Hoodie Man could be my old sales manager Rags.

My favorite bartender thinks I'm too dizzy to drive myself home, so it's after midnight when Solana and Luis drop me off at my condo. Luis even insists on accompanying me to the door. My Florsheims drag on the brick-lined cement walkway like flat tires. I whiff a taste of my neighbor's cat litter.

"You should remain in your bed all of tomorrow," Luis says.

Lacking the strength to verbalize, I nod, unlock my door and walk into the dark living room. There's noise, and I know something's wrong even before I click the light switch.

Oh, hell no.

Beth and a young man I recognize as my old neighbor Mike both rise from a previously unseen and decidedly compromising position on my nine-foot leather couch. Beth's fingers rush to the undone buttons on her blouse. "Shit," she says.

Bare-chested Mike appears only slightly older than Beth. Some kind of caveman instinct speaks to me about trying to choke him, but basically, there is nothing going on here I didn't do myself at their age. I mean, everybody's still wearing their pants.

"Get your clothes on, son," I say. "Time to go home."

Mike bends to snatch his floor-mounted sweatshirt. My pulse tick-tocks higher when he unfolds the exact style sweatshirt Hoodie Man wore while assaulting me three hours ago. Mike's about the right size, too. True I thought it was Rags. Yes, gray is a common color for hoodies, but the zipper is even torn. And dangling.

Mike pulls the gray sweatshirt over his head, pausing for a moment to show me his muscled chest before tugging down the bottom. If I had muscles like Mike, maybe I'd pose, too. Could he be the guy who punched me in Luis' parking lot?

"You two been here for a while?" I ask.

Both are speechless.

I nod toward Mike. "I was assaulted a few hours ago by a guy your size, in a hoodie like yours—right down to the torn zipper."

"Daddy!"

My daughter is embarrassed. I can tell. Her father must be the dumbest man alive.

"The zippers on those hoodies *always* tear," Beth says. "He's seventeen years old and grew up on our street. How could you *possibly* think he's the one who mugged you?"

I don't know. How could I?

TWELVE

Besides being tall, athletic, German and blond, Randall Zimmer III, Esquire, grows seriously antagonistic wrinkles between his eyebrows whenever he frowns. That, the short hair and overall butch good looks could win him movie roles as Nazi villains should he ever want to change occupations.

"You invested your life savings—twenty thousand dollars—in risky options, one week before the merger, and you expect the SEC to believe you didn't believe it was inside information?"

We're in Zimmer's Branchtown headquarters, Mr. Z seated behind a hand-carved antique desk roughly the size of Vic's private office at Carr Securities. His joined hands rest on the polished teak surface, both index fingers coming together at the tip, pointing at me. A yellow number eight pencil bounces back and forth between his thumbs.

Reminds me of my high school principal.

"I didn't buy the options," I say. "The trades are in my account, but Mr. Vic did the trading—without my knowledge. He set me up."

Zimmer stares at my face. "Why would he do that—trade in your account?"

"Because I took away control of the company from him last year. If he gets me tossed out of the business, my license revoked, I'd be forced to sell—and at a bargain price, too."

"So you had no pre-announcement knowledge of this merger?"

I look at the ceiling. "Absolutely not." I can't tell Zimmer the truth. It might cloud his judgment. More importantly, he's an officer of the court and can't present false evidence. "This whole problem belongs to Mr. Vic."

Zimmer uses the number eight pencil to check his notes. We're preparing for our upcoming appearance before the SEC and the U.S. District Attorney for New York. The subpoena suggests I'll be answering a lot of the same questions for both agencies of the Federal government. As Mr. Z explained, the SEC is considering civil action, while the DA for New York will review possible criminal charges.

"You called him Mr. Vic," Zimmer says. "You're talking about your partner, Vic Bonacelli, recently assaulted and still in a coma?"

"That's him."

Zimmer's frown is back. "Without his testimony, it will be difficult to prove he was responsible for the purchases in your account."

I can't think of a snappy answer to that one. In fact, I can hardly think at all. The truth is so glaringly nasty: That I *didn't* buy those options might be impossible to prove.

Standing up, I say, "I'll check out the company's records, talk to the back office, see what I can come up with."

"Hire a computer expert. It would be advantageous to present evidence as to which computer terminal those trades originated from—provided it wasn't yours, of course."

"Of course."

"One more thing," Zimmer says. "Do you have any friends or associates in Las Vegas?"

"Vegas? Not that I can think of."

Mr. Z offers me his hand. "Good," he says. "But think hard over the next twenty-four hours. Check your telephone book and your address book. Your Christmas card list. Let me know if there's anyone in Vegas. It's important that I know if you do."

"Why? What's with Vegas?"

"Las Vegas is where this investigation is centered," Zimmer says. "According to people I know at the SEC, there are individuals from Las Vegas who each made over one million dollars on Fishman call options—options purchased one day before the merger announcement."

To Mama Bones, Eddie Flukes looks a little shabby. As if he's not taking good care of himself since his mother died. Eddie's pants are shiny in the seat and the knees. His hair is too long and his fingernails are dirty. Even this old Asbury Park diner where Eddie wanted to meet does not say reassuring things. The place has been a junkie hangout since the 1950s.

"You want me to investigate your own kid?" Eddie Flukes says.

"Not investigate—check something out," Mama Bones says. "How you doing since your mama died, Eddie. Everything okay?"

"I'm fine. Better than Vic, I hear. You already know who shot him?"

"No. What do you mean, better than Vic? Who says?"

"Didn't he get shot?"

"Yeah, he got shot. But he's okay. He's gonna be fine. And you have balls saying you're doing better than the guy who owns his own business, who took your starting linebacker job and your girlfriend when he was just a freshman."

"Sorry, Mama Bones. Christ. That was thirty years ago."

Poor Eddie. Mama Bones sighs. She has not been herself. "No, I'm-a the one should be sorry. I'm having a bad day, Eddie. Heck, I'm having a lot of bad days since Vic got shot. I apologize."

He shakes his head, like Mama Bones is getting old and crazy.

"Forget I said that stuff, okay?" she says. "I know things aren't easy for you since your mama passed. I want to give you a job, ask you to talk to my Vic's friends. I think he kept some secrets."

Eddie nods, his long hair falling forward over his ears. "How about the jeweler's briefcase Tomas mentioned? Want me to see if I can find out where it came from, what was inside?"

"Sure, why not? That's-a the thing that makes me think Vic's got secrets."

"Tomas also said maybe I'd be looking for Patricia Willis."

"If you see her, sure. I'll pay you. We hear she talked to the cops before she disappeared. Me, Tomas and Gianni are looking for her—she's maybe a witness, the first person we gotta talk to if we want to find out who shot Vic. Can't hurt having an extra set of eyeballs."

Eddie nods and fingers the inside collar of his dirty shirt. What's he worried about?

"How are you getting along with Bluefish's replacement?" he asks.

Mama Bones studies Eddie's face. "The Turk? Ha. Me and him go way back—all the way to Asbury Park High School."

"No problems, huh? I hear The Turk thinks you might be a rival."

"That's funny," Mama Bones says. "Although, now I think about it, the Turk always was afraid of girls."

She stands up. "Time to go. You wanna buy the coffee, or you want me to pay the check, deduct it from your fee?"

The next afternoon at Carr Securities, Carmela asks me—Austin Carr, the company's majority stockholder—to help box some of Mr. Vic's personal items. She wants to surround her father in the hospital with familiar knick-knacks in hopes of waking him from the coma. I'm appalled she wants me to perform physical labor, especially on the promise good luck charms might accomplish where science has failed. But since removing Vic from deep sleep means he would be available for a grilling by my attorney, and would boost the company's sales production, I unbutton my silk tie and roll up the sleeves on my Brooks Brothers button-down collar white shirt.

In the process of helping Carmela pack things, I reach for the four-inch tall, polished stone bull Mr. Vic likes to rub when stocks are crashing. Vic believes massaging the realistically carved miniature black and horned animal will make stock buyers return to the market. As I grasp Vic's idol of greed, my fingers snag on something sharp underneath. "Ouch."

Carmela isn't listening. She's reading the back of an old photo. I flip the stone bull upside down, see a black plastic tape attached to the animal's belly. The tape holds a tiny metal object the size of two sugar cubes. My gut tenses. Looks like a listening device.

Carmela pays no attention. I tear the device off and slip it into my pocket.

Thirty five minutes later I'm in a strip mall off White Street showing my recently discovered snooping device to a nineteen-year-old techno boy, his long surfer hair and implied expertise standing behind the counter at Branchtown's local TV Hut franchise. "What is this thing...exactly?" I ask.

"Let's see," he says. His fingers peel off the black tape. "Advantage Security makes this—a microphone and the battery pack. It's super sensitive. You can hear a whisper."

The kid could be playing hooky from high school. He's tall, a beanpole, with shaggy blond hair and ears the size of Trenton; gawky, like he couldn't walk across the room without knocking something over.

"We sell these," he says. "You want one like it?"

"No. Can you tell me if you sold this particular one? I see it has a serial number."

His eyes check the floor for mice.

"Would twenty bucks help my cause?" I say.

I clean and jerk a green Andrew Jackson from my wallet, slide the bill onto the counter. There's no one close by, but this kid is probably too embarrassed to take the money.

Junior snags my twenty, a blur of Jersey hand speed. "Be right back," he says.

He might be more sophisticated than I thought. That, or he actually grew up right here in central Jersey, where breeding, education and looks mean little. Around here, cash is king.

One other customer occupies the store. He's in the back, checking pre-paid telephone services—a senior citizen in long sleeves and suspenders focusing on his planned purchase. Pops doesn't know I exist. Outside in the strip mall parking lot, an eighteen-wheel supermarket truck rumbles past. The TV Hut's front plate glass window flutters. A cloud of brown diesel exhaust follows the truck through the parking lot like a shadow.

The tall awkward kid shuffles back to me at the front counter. His hands are empty, the big-knuckles swinging back and forth across his boney thighs.

"We sold it two weeks ago," he says.

"Got a name for me?"

His long face feigns concern. "I could get fired."

"How about another twenty?"

"Make it a hundred," he says. "I had to check the credit card receipts."

"You already looked up the name?"

"Yeah. I checked for another guy yesterday. Charged him two hundred."

"Another guy like me? Older, younger?"

"Older, I think. He kept his face turned. Wore a coat and hat. So you want the name of the person who bought this Advantage bug for one hundred, or not?"

I consider my situation, the value of one hundred American smackers. A very good dinner for two, with wine. Two cartons of New Jersey cigarettes. The answer to a question you are dying to know.

I count out five more Andrew Jacksons.

The name the kid writes for me on a slip of paper—the guy who bought the listening device—is Rags, Thomas Ragsdale.

THIRTEEN

I key the Camry's engine. Too late to start hunting for Rags in north Jersey. What good would confronting the lying bastard do anyway? I know what he did, the stuff *I said* he could have heard and recorded. Also, pretty sure he was wearing the hoodie, punching me in Luis' parking lot, asking me where's the cash. Maybe it's over-confidence, but if I carefully consider his rat brain a few minutes, I believe Rags' reasoning will come to me. The man has always been easy to figure. More unsettling is the older man who also visited TV Hut, who also knows about Rags and his listening device.

Who was that?

I head back to my condo amid the sounds of Branchtown's Friday rush hour—horns, engines and squealing moms with kids. Every traffic jam on Front Street begins at St. Theresa's combined grammar and high schools.

From my bedroom phone, I call Beth. Earlier she said she'd be going to her girlfriend Janie's house after school, and in fact she's there when I call, happy and alert, working on an English research paper the two young women were assigned as a team. I can hear Janie, someone outside mowing a lawn. Since I know the family, and because I also talk to Janie's mother, I say yes when Beth asks to spend the night.

I drop my tie and shoes on the familiar gray tweed carpet, jump on my bed. I'm too tired to take off my shirt and pants. Beyond tired. I'm exhausted, the kind of beat that makes you weak, when fear and sadness bubble up from the past and taunt you with past mistakes. The bed cuddles me like cotton candy, but I can't stop listening to the crap in my head. My list of troubles seems endless: There's my junior partner who's trying to get me tossed from the business. Vic's been shot, and lies in a coma. How about the woman I might be in love with, Patricia, missing since Vic's shooting? I know love is a strong word to use so quickly but I have never experienced anything like the feelings I have for Patricia. And since lust is practically my middle name, what else could this be? The feelings are new, overpowering and consuming. If I did not have children, I do not think my life would hold any other interest right now. I swear. Patricia and her freckles are practically all I can think about. Another thing—I could easily be charged with insider trading next month when I talk to the Securities and Exchange Commission and the U.S. District Attorney for New York. Nice for the kids if their daddy's alleged crimes hit the newspaper. What else? Oh, yeah. My worst enemy, Rags, might have the raw material to create phony evidence against me, take my securities license and my livelihood. And what else did Rags hear with his little piece of spy equipment? What did he mean, "Where's the cash?"

I study the stucco ceiling until it's too dark to see.

The sun wakes me gently, its warm golden light sliced into diagonal stripes by the window blinds above my head. I'm in a much better mood than when I went to sleep, so maybe my problems were illusions of fatigue. Probably not, but things still feel better. I roll onto my side, establish bare feet on carpet and shuffle into a steaming shower, looking forward to my Saturday morning ritual of grinding coffee beans for an extra-big pot. I can hear in my head an ancient Ink Spots tune my father used to play on plastic record disks as big as Frisbees: *I like coffee, I like tea. I like the java jive and it likes me.*

A thump from inside my condo lights a spark on my spinal column. Something fell in the kitchen, a relatively small and light item—a nearly insignificant thing, say like my retirement fund. I'm a statue, my head and one arm wearing a clean T-shirt, the other arm reaching inside the stretched cotton to find the shirt's other arm hole. Half a straight jacket for a half crazy man.

I wait for another sound, and ten seconds later I get one, a squeaky footstep on my kitchen tile. I take three deep breaths in preparation for combat. Oxygenating my blood. Ha. Where's my Captain Stockbroker uniform? Quietly, I get my arm through and pull the T-shirt over my head. I don't like guns, and would never keep one at home because of the children. But right now I wish an AK-47 rested under my bed instead of a baseball bat. That Vargas guy is more than I can handle.

I hit over three hundred in high school, however, and know how to use the aluminum swatter I snatch from the floor. Gripping my Willie Mays Autographed Model with both hands, I tiptoe into the hall, halfway down the corridor and stop. Four or five more paces will bring the half of the kitchen alcove into view on my right, the sofa and TV on the left. I'm waiting for another noise. My lizard brain needs one more reading to accurately program the thrust of my bat. All I hear is my own heart.

Enough time passes, I wonder if I dreamed the whole thing, or heard a neighbor move a piece of furniture. Then someone—a person—shifts their weight in my kitchen.

Four fast strides put me at the end of the hall. No one is visible in the kitchen, at least above the counter. I can't see the floor. In the living area, a teak lamp is lighted when I'd turned it off. I snap my gaze back to the kitchen. My programmable Mr. Coffee is running. The green light's on. I smell the Colombian...

From a low place behind the kitchen counter, an odd human shape rises into view. My gut dives off a cliff, then parachutes to safety when I recognize Patricia in black eyeliner, fake lashes, purple lipstick, and a new hairdo—five-inch long, silver tipped spikes.

"Good morning, sweet talker," she says. "Ready for coffee?"

My hand covers my chest in mock despair, though the ticker is definitely pounding. Patricia wears a sleeveless black halter top with a short black-leather skirt. Her belt and necklace are made of razorblade dog chain.

"How did you get in?" I ask.

She shows me a key on the chain around her neck. "You gave it to me, remember?"

Actually, I'd forgotten. My hands tingle to touch her and I half run around the kitchen bar to grab her. Her body crushes against mine, warm and giving. "Are you okay?" I say. "I've been worried."

"I'm good. Scared, but good."

Her weight comes against me fully, her flesh pressing in special places. Powerful emotions and predictable physical responses develop. But what I notice most is the electricity. I don't remember this kind of thing before. Even the first year with Susan when I *thought* I was in love. The air around Patricia and me buzzes when we touch.

"What's with the dominatrix look?" I say.

"It's a disguise. The guy who shot Vic shot at me, too."

"You saw it was a man? How about his face?"

"I *heard* him more than I saw him. He rang my apartment doorbell ten minutes after you left. Vic opened the door like he was expecting someone, and then—bang, bang—Vic stumbled backward and fell."

"Jeez."

"Two bloody spots in the middle of his chest. Red on white. I can still see it."

Patricia pushes tighter against me, lays her head on my shoulder. I want to wrap up this woman like a birthday gift or a Christmas package, let the electricity between us warm my soul until all human fear goes away. I want an end to that cold loneliness I felt last night when I went to bed.

"When did the guy shoot at you?" I ask.

She leans back from my chest to look at me. The spikes in her hair tickle my cheek.

"He stood in the entrance, with Vic lying there. Told me to throw him the briefcase. So I did. Hard, too—right at his head. When he ducked, I ran for the back door."

So it *was* Vic's briefcase Mr. Hoodie—maybe Rags—punched me about in Luis' parking. "Smart. And that's when he shot at you?"

"Right. I felt the bullet fly past my head before I heard the shot, honest to God. It splintered the door jamb the same second I ran through."

"Did he keep the briefcase?"

"Yes. How did you know?"

"Remember that guy I told you about, Tom Ragsdale, my former sales manager?"

She nods.

"He knows about the briefcase. He had a hoodie on, but I'm sure it was him. He sucker punched me in Luis' parking lot, asked me where the cash was—the cash in the *briefcase*."

Silence.

I remove myself from Patricia's embrace. The coffee smells good, plus if I don't let go soon I might try something rude. My favorite coffee mug—Bugs Bunny inside a Merry Melodies yellow circle—waits for me in the cupboard.

"If this man Rags has the briefcase," Patricia says, "then he's the guy who shot Vic and took my ruby."

"Ruby?" I say. "What ruby?"

FOURTEEN

Patricia ushers me to a chair at my own kitchen table. She is about to explain why my former boss, now my junior partner and rival for Patricia's affections, Mr. Vic possessed a ruby while being shot inside her apartment. Should be a fun story.

"Vic and I had a relationship for twelve years, sweet talker. Before I explain about the ruby, you need to understand Vic and I have been lovers a long time. But remember, I dumped him for you after one day on the beach."

I pour myself a cup from the coffee pot. "You loved him?"

"Still do," Patricia says, "for what he is. A good old friend, a romantic bullshitter. But I wasn't *in* love with him anymore. Not for six months, maybe longer."

"You told him about us?"

"How could I deny it? I'd just brought you home."

I glance outside my condo's kitchen window at a maple tree, its few remaining leaves orange and yellow while my gut turns hot and green. This woman keeps surprising me, saying things that change the landscape. I don't like hearing about Patricia and Mr. Vic. I don't like to think about her and another man. When did I get like this? I hardly know this woman.

"So what's this ruby?" I ask.

"It's my commission for my brother's information. It's what was inside that briefcase you saw when we came to my place."

"Pretty big briefcase for a ruby."

"Pretty big ruby, but the briefcase also had a lot of cash at one time, Vic said, but not when he showed me."

"How big a ruby?" I ask.

"So big it has a name—the Big Mojo. It was part of an even larger ruby discovered in Africa over a hundred years ago, then smuggled out in two pieces. One piece—Big Mojo—

was cut, sold, then stolen and sold again within its first year in Havana."

I sip my coffee. "Okay. So Vic made a pile somehow on Fishman stock, obviously, because he paid you off. Not in cash, but with a big ruby he had some great stories about. Are you sure Big Mojo wasn't a proposal of marriage? Maybe he was shot before he could ask the question."

"Vic told me twelve years ago he would never break up his family. Like I said, I think he went overboard trying to keep his *comare*—me, especially since his rival was you."

I stare at my coffee.

"I know Vic," Patricia says. "The ruby was a show, at first I thought for me. But him carrying the gun, what he said to you when we came home, that tells me the ruby wasn't about his love for me. It was about his own ego."

"Did he say where he got the ruby?"

"A friend of his introduced him to people in Vegas," Patricia says. "Vic said Big Mojo was part of a heist that...you know...fell off the truck."

Las Vegas, the city of inside traders, according to my attorney.

"Too bad the ruby was in the briefcase when I threw it at the guy's head," Patricia says. "Think the man in the hoodie was really your ex sales manager Rags?"

"It looked like him, but I don't know for sure." I open the fridge and show Patricia a carton of eggs. "You want some breakfast?"

"Sounds good. Mind if I hang around here today?" Patricia says. "The police were finished yesterday investigating their crime scene, but I couldn't hire anyone to clean up Vic's blood until this afternoon."

"Stay as long as you like. But I'm not sure you'll be safe while I'm at work and Beth's in school. Whether it's Rags or someone else, Hoodie Man knows a lot about me—where I hang out, probably where I live."

She slips her arms around me. "I'm safe."

Mama Bones loves the new office part of her basement kitchen—sitting at a desk behind a door she can lock—but she hates using the stupid computer. She can't figure out the darn thing. Like what is a spreadsheet. Sounds like dirty laundry at a sex motel. Mama Bones has been writing down her weekly bet totals on a piece of paper for twenty-seven years.

"This computer program sucks," she says.

Gianni shakes his head. "You going to keep complaining about the new boss' reporting requirements, or you want to hear what Eddie Flukes called about?"

Couldn't be much info or Gianni would have already said. "Sure," Mama Bones says. "Tell me."

"Patricia has been smart. He hasn't picked up a lead yet. But Eddie *did* dig up something on Vic."

Mama Bones takes her gaze off the computer screen. "What?"

"Eddie says Vic was working a deal with people in Las Vegas."

"People?"

"Business people," Gianni says. "*Our thing* business people."

Mama Bones shakes her head. "No way Vic would work Our Thing without telling me."

"Eddie says he did, that Vic used your name."

"My Vic knows he *has* to come through me for that."

"Eddie said his information was confirmed. Tom Ragsdale even blurted about it in front of one of our bookies. Vic arranged some deal in Vegas he didn't tell you about."

"What would Vic hide from his own mother, huh? And how would that drug addict Tommy Ragsdale know?"

"Eddie doesn't know yet but I bet he will after he talks to Ragsdale."

Mama Bones checks the clock in the upper right of her computer screen, pushes back from her desk to snatch her purse off the back of the chair. "Why wait? Let's go ask Tommy ourselves. He's all alone on the night shift in one hour."

Gianni doesn't look happy. Tough.

"Come on," she says. "Thirty-five, forty minutes up the Parkway."

Inside the night watchman's tiny office at the industrial bakery, Tommy Ragsdale tied up in a chair, Mama Bones stares at Carmela's ex-husband—his throat in particular—as she reaches for the hunting knife. Gianni put a nice big blade on the table.

Tommy's eyes get real big—like a little boy watching a horror show. It's a mean thing she's doing, sure. But this bastard used to hit her granddaughter.

"Don't worry, Tommy," she says. "I'm not going to stab or torture you." Mama Bones smiles. "You used to be family."

She watches hope flicker in Tommy's eyes.

"We're going to shoot you," she says.

She nods at Gianni, and her nephew shows Tommy the big Sig Sauer. Gianni says it's a P226 X-FIVE, but Mama Bones thinks he should call it Truth Serum. Looks like a hand-held cannon.

Tommy moans. Mama Bones would feel sorry for him if he hadn't beat up Carmela once a week the whole time they were together. Two black eyes and a broken cheek bone in less than three months. If she thinks about it too much, Mama Bones feels like using the knife to cut off his balls.

She says, "That is, we gonna shoot you with that Sig Sauer if you don't tell me what I want to know. Okay?"

Tommy nods. Happy now he's still got a chance.

"My boy Vic was doing business with people in Las Vegas," Mama Bones says, "and I want to know who these people are."

"The only name I know is Santo Vargas," Tommy says. "I heard Vic mention the name in his office."

Gianni thumb-cocks the Sig's hammer, then brings the gun closer—until the barrel touches Tommy's nose. Mama Bones hopes Tommy or Gianni don't sneeze. "We don't believe you," she says. "You know more than you're telling."

His eyes bulge. His upper lip spouts beads of sweat. He's going to say more now for sure. "I know Santo Vargas brought Vic's payoff from the Vegas people," Tommy says. "Vic's payoff for information he gave them. But there was something else Vargas wanted to do while he was in town."

"What?"

"I don't know."

"How you know *any* of these things, huh? Vic tell you?"

"No," Tommy says.

"Then you know one of these guys in Vegas?"

"No. The only guy I know from Vegas is Santo Vargas."

"So you know this guy Vargas? You contacted him for Vic?"

"No, no, Mama Bones. I would have told you, asked your permission. Vic used someone else to contact them, maybe that ex-cop Mallory. I know they had a meeting."

Mama Bones glances at Gianni. "My Vic didn't talk to you anymore, I know. How come you know so much? How you know about Santo Vargas?"

Tommy swallows hard. His Adam's apple looks like a stuffed baby chicken. "I bugged Vic's office."

FIFTEEN

The clock says 9:50 AM when I plop down at the sales desk Monday morning. Carr Securities buzzes with activity. Stocks are crashing. Pink message slips cover the space around my black desk model telephone like plastic flamingos washed up after a hurricane. One of the pink notes is from Beth's school. I snatch the telephone, jam the receiver against my left ear and dial. "This is Austin Carr. I'm returning Mrs. Osborne's call."

"Oh, yes, Mr. Carr. Can you hold one second?"

Carmela's watching me, attracted to my conversation I suppose by the tone of my voice. Yes, I'm worried. The change in my daughter's attitudes and appearance troubles me, not to mention making out half-naked with Mike the Muscleman on my couch.

I stand up, spin my back on the sales floor to face the green chalkboard where our trading department advertises our product specials to the floor salesmen. We have a first-rate hot issue today, a fast-dwindling block of tax-free bonds from the State of Jersey. The bonds are a safe haven during stock market crashes.

"Mr. Carr?"

"Is my daughter okay?" I say.

Ms. Osborne clears her throat. Hesitating. I want to scream at her.

"Your daughter ran out of English class this morning, and I'm afraid no one's seen her since."

My gut wiggles and squirms. "Why would she run out of class? What happened?"

"The teacher asked two of her friends. They had no explanation."

"I don't understand, Ms. Osborne. Something must have happened. Beth's never done anything like this before."

"Well...actually..."

"What?"

"She cut two morning classes last week. She tried to claim she was sick and had a doctor's appointment, but later she admitted she had been smoking in the park with another student."

"Mike Branigan?"

"No, it wasn't Michael."

"Okay, Ms. Osborne. Thanks. You'll call me if you see her?"

"Of course."

I hold down the button, then let go to punch up Susan's number. The ex-wife's stopped working now that Bob the Dentist moved in. I reach her at their home.

"Have you heard from Beth?" I ask.

"She stumbled in here ten minutes ago," she says.

Thank God. Oh, thank God. "Is she all right?"

"Your daughter is high as a kite. She admitted she's been drinking and smoking pot since eight this morning at some girl's house. They've started a band."

"Great."

"Nice job, Dad. How long did you have her, a week?"

"Excuse me?"

"She never did anything like this with me."

"Yeah? Well, she didn't start dyeing her hair and dressing wild at *my* house."

"I think I'll be keeping Beth here with me for the foreseeable future. And Bob wanted me to ask, did you hire a private detective to watch our house?"

"No need. I get detailed reports from Ryan."

"There's been a black SUV parked across the street all day."

"Probably the FBI," I say. "They have a few questions about Bob's overactive prescription pad."

"Very funny. But you'd better cut back on the jokes and ramp up the father act, Austin. Our daughter is floundering in the deep end."

I hate it when Susan's right. My day becomes dark and cloudy.

"Can I talk to her?" I say.

"She lying down."

"Put her on the phone. You're the one who wants me to act like a father."

"All right. Hang on."

Below me on the sales floor, Bobby G pulls off his one-ear headset and hoots like a hockey fan. "A hundred of the Jersey G.O.s," he says.

Bobby's just sold one hundred thousand dollars face value of those Jersey bonds, part of a new issue to help finance the state's unfunded pension liabilities. I hear Beth pick up the telephone. Bobby's gross commission will be seven hundred and fifty bucks. The house gets forty percent of that.

"Hi, Daddy. Do you want to yell at me, too?"

Beth sounds tired.

"This behavior is going to get you in big trouble," I say. "To me it shows how immature you are."

"I'm not the little girl you think."

"Ditching school to smoke pot proves you are, toots. More important, sixteen is still a child in the eyes of the law."

"Only because of a criminally corrupt political system."

"Excuse me?"

"Don't pretend you're not aware of the NSA's spying, the CIA's interest in heroin to finance their secret assassinations, subjugation of the poor by corporate warlords, and the—"

"Whoa, whoa, honey. I'm talking about sixteen-year-old children—kids making decisions they might not be mature enough to make."

"What would you know? Stockbrokers are bottom feeders of a greedy capitalist structure."

To most people, she has a point. Robbers like Bernie Madoff grab all the headlines by ripping off the wealthy and famous, while the rest of us investment guys do the best we can helping manage money for the retirement plans of cops, health aides, social workers, and teachers. People the media doesn't honestly care about.

Having Beth back at her mother's is no solution for my daughter's problems, but selfishly, her absence does have a positive side: Patricia and I can now explore our new relationship with more privacy and intimacy. I head home from the office hoping Patricia might cook me my favorite dinner.

My front door ajar, I push inside. One of the living room table lamps lies on the carpet, and the black lacquered Asian coffee table rests on its side. My pulse jumps as the crash of breaking glass rattles down the hall from the spare bedroom. Beth is safe at home with her mom. But Patricia...

My coat slides off my arm as I run through the living room, Florsheims thudding on the carpet. Thinking Santo Vargas could be waiting for me, I hit the not-quite-shut, spare bedroom doorway running. The slab of wood flies open, bangs the wall. The bedroom-office is empty, but the sliding glass door is cracked, the frame off its slider. Outside, my patio flowers and plants have been trampled. The gate is wide open.

I reach the sidewalk to see the ex-cop James Mallory stuffing Patricia into the back seat of a black Ford Explorer. Her hands and mouth are bound in silver tape. Why did I let Patricia stay with me? I knew it wasn't safe. And why the hell is Mallory taking her? He must be Mr. Hoodie, or maybe the older man who also visited TV Hut.

Mallory takes off. My keys are still in my hand. I jog thirty-five yards to my Camry and fire up. I get lucky at the first intersection, glimpsing Mallory's Explorer wheeling right onto Front Street. There's a car coming. I have to wait. And while a bright crimson Mercedes whizzes past me, while my Camry's engine hums patiently, I realize I am in love with Patricia Willis. I *know* this because my heart is pounding and my skin is wet with perspiration. I am about to chase a man who might harm me, and though I fully experience the fear, I am resolute to the task. I will risk life and limb for Patricia Willis. With no hesitation. I do this easily and naturally because I love her.

Pretty sure, anyway.

SIXTEEN

Keeping the red Mercedes between my Camry and the black Explorer, I chase Mallory east through Fair Haven and Rumson toward the ocean. Only the two of us turn left at the Sea Bright bridge, however, and quickly I'm too close going north on Ocean Avenue. If Mallory sees me, loses me, I might never see Patricia again. Mallory kidnapping Patricia *has* to be about that ruby and Vic being shot.

Of course, why a stockbroker like me is chasing bad guys remains a mystery. Is there a badge on my chest? A cape on my back? A weapon of any kind with which to defend myself or rescue Patricia? No. Maybe I'm not in love. Maybe I'm nuts. The thought has occurred to me. How can I love someone I've just met? Infatuation, for sure. The whole thing is shiny and wonderful and hot red. But love? I wonder if we could trust each other with our lives, should the situation call for it. Or put the other one first in our thoughts for a time during sickness.

But if this *feels* like love, to the point of risking bodily harm, then what's the difference? What is *real* love? All sensations share a problem of durability.

I drop back as our vehicles navigate the three mile straightaway between the Sea Bright bridge and the entrance to Sandy Hook park. On my right, a cemented stone retaining wall keeps back the new, piped-in sand and an ever-hungry Atlantic Ocean. I think about dialing Luis for help, but remember my cell phone rests inside my sport jacket, the coat lying where I dropped it fifteen minutes ago on my living room floor.

I wait until the Explorer crests the top of the off-ramp before following Mallory onto the five-mile sand bar that is Sandy Hook, a unit of the America's Gateway National Recreation Area. The park charges for automobiles during the summer season, but it's free access the rest of the year.

I'm worried Mallory brought Patricia here to do her harm. Sandy Hook represents much of Gateway's twenty-six thousand acres of wilderness, a major rest stop for millions of migrating birds, and the United States' park system's only wildlife refuge. Once summer passes and the beaches lose their draw, there are few less populated areas. Like Jersey's Pine Barrens in the south and Wetlands to the north, Sandy Hook is a terrific place to unofficially and criminally bury your dead.

The road out the Sandy Hook peninsula doesn't fork until two-thirds of the way to the end. It's easy to stay back of the Explorer, out of Mallory's sight, but close enough to follow his SUV's headlights. His high beams throw a bright shine on the roadside holly and scrub pine. If he's looking in his mirror, I don't think he'll notice my parking lights half a mile behind him. It's hard to see, but I do okay hugging the double line.

Near the end of the peninsula's north-south road, we fork to the right, then turn hard right again to approach rows of cement and rusted-iron artillery bunkers. Since the American Revolution, Sandy Hook has been home for serious gun battlements—a major part of New York City's defense system. These particular ruins, which aimed big guns at the entrance to New York Harbor, date from World War II.

I follow Mallory to the extreme north end of the peninsula and a flat expanse of broken pavement the size of Giant Stadium parking. I flick off my parking lights and stay back a quarter-mile while Mallory weaves across the moonlit asphalt with patches of cement. Weeds grow between the cracks, some four feet tall.

Near the end of the flat pavement Mallory brakes against a row of old telephone poles, a barrier marking the entrance to North Beach's blocks-long foot trail to the sand and water. The beach path runs along a fenced off U.S. Coast Guard training and living facility that includes the whole northern tip of Sandy Hook. Coast Guard lights let me see the Explorer, the trailhead and another SUV, a Chevy, parked nose-forward next to Mallory.

There's a familiar shape inside. A man.

I flash back two summers ago when Ryan and I were here with the Cub Scouts. There's a fork not far up the trail, one path that leads to the beach, a second that heads for a two-story observation platform. Built decades earlier, birders use the tower all year, but particularly in early fall because of migrating birds of prey. Photographers snap shots of the Verrazano Bridge or the heavy ship traffic all year long. Ryan, the Cub Scouts and I mainly killed time so Mom could go shopping.

The interior lights of Mallory's Explorer flash on and so do the Chevy's when Mallory rolls outside to greet the other driver: It's Rags—Tommy Ragsdale—my ex sales manager and newly declared mortal enemy.

What do these guys want with Patricia?

Mama Bones hands Gianni the Nikon binoculars. Her body hurts in certain places. She needs to work out again, exercise more. The busted up World War II cement bunker is a nice place for her and Gianni to watch Sandy's North Beach parking lot and Rags, but the climb was nasty from where Gianni hid his Jeep. As a place to sit and wait, the rutted broken concrete bites ass.

"That's two-hundred you owe me," Mama Bones says. "I asked you, why would Rags sit there quiet if he wasn't waiting for somebody."

Gianni takes the binoculars off his eyeballs, stands and offers Mama Bones his hand. "Yeah, you win. I could have sworn he was waiting for dark to get rid of a body. The way he backed against the trail. Want to move closer?"

"Yeah. Let's see who gets out of that Explorer."

They've been following Rags all day, Mama Bones hoping Carmela's ex will lead them to the briefcase and Vic's shooter—if it wasn't Rags himself.

Gianni adjusts the Nikons. "There's somebody else in the parking lot. A Camry with its lights off."

"A Camry? Oh, Mother Mary."

"No," Gianni says. "It's Austin Carr. He must have been following the Explorer."

***

To the right of my Camry, birds squabble for a night's roost inside a stand of dying pine trees. Low-lying evergreens on the shore were killed or damaged by Hurricane Sandy back in 2012, and this miniature petrified forest nestled on the perimeter of the paved expanse provides a place to stay out of sight, wait for my chance to rescue Patricia.

Say what?

What am I doing? What is there about the stockbroker experience and training that prepares me for physical and mortal combat? I take a deep breath and think one more time. My head and gut agree my genetic duty belongs to my children and their future. I should not be out on deserted Sandy Hook, risking my health for Patricia Willis or anybody else who isn't family. However; there are times when the head and the gut don't count. Sometimes you have to go with your heart, see what happens—even if that foolish red organ sends you over Niagara Falls in a barrel.

And there is no denying right now, for better or worse, for richer or poorer, for as long as this love shall last, my heart belongs to Patricia Willis.

I switch off the Camry's overhead before I slide outside. My fingers shut the car door with the same firm gentleness I guide a woman on the dance floor. A few hundred yards away, the Atlantic breaks and washes against Sandy Hook's northern shore, a rolling swish against the quiet. Icy wind gusts off the water and stings my skin. The air tastes of salt.

Mallory drags Patricia between the two SUVs. I'm coming, getting closer by the second, crouch-jogging along the perimeter of the park-sized lot. Patricia's mouth is still taped. Her wrists, too. I slow my gait, then freeze when Rags scans the dark in my direction—as if he's heard my scuffles on the broken asphalt.

Rags knows about Patricia and the ruby because he eavesdropped on Vic's telephone conversations. I'm considering if Mallory's involvement could be anything but the TV Hut—listening device angle, when Rags grabs Patricia's shoulders and Mallory takes her knees. They lift and carry her like a rug delivery team toward the entrance to the nature trail—the same path I walked two summers ago with Ryan and his Cub Scout Troop.

I'm still thirty yards from the two SUVs, but fence lights from the Coast Guard station let me glimpse Mallory and Rags carry Patricia past the wooden barriers to the trailhead. Among the wild holly and scrub pine, their individual shapes gradually become a single, shifting blob of shadow.

I jog, my mind mulling over the previous trip here with Ryan: Four or five hundred yards up the same trail Mallory and Rags began to carry Patricia is North Beach, where from the surf you can stare across seven miles of Atlantic Ocean—from Jersey to Coney Island, New York—and the geological entrance to New York Harbor.

The Coast Guard facility helps, but following Rags and Mallory with no flashlight, I'm pretty much in the dark.

The story of my life.

SEVENTEEN

For hopefully the last time, I ask myself what I'm doing, sneaking toward a battle with two grown men. Rags maybe I can handle. But Mallory is an ex-cop and former Marine. In a confrontation with both, my *survival* could be claimed a major victory. Whether real love or infatuation, this screwball thing I have for Patricia could easily get me killed.

When I reach the fork in the trail—one to the beach, one to the bird platform—the clouds break, and moonlight fades the shadows around me. I stop to listen. Wind hisses in the tree tops. The ocean attacks a sandy shore. Then, to the right—toward the bird tower—whispering and the scratch of shuffling feet begin an all-male conversation that quickly becomes an argument.

The wind makes some words clear, others not, but anger is certain. Rags yells something about "a fake," and Mallory speaks Vargas' name in the same breath as "the aluminum briefcase." There is more scuffling of feet and Rags yells, his voice moving, falling. A single pair of feet is already clambering noisily down the tower steps.

The bird platform is only two stories tall, but it sounded like Mallory threw Rags off. Did he throw Patricia, too? My fingers close into fists as I jog down the path toward the tower, pulling my knees up high with each stride, an ancient warrior's technique I learned reading Carlos Castaneda. Reduces the risk of tripping when you can't see what's in front of you. Hey, everybody has to believe in something. Faith is always better than fear.

Someone's running toward me on the same trail, coming *from* the bird tower. Light feet, short strides—stopwatch clicks between the washing of surf and my own clomping. I drop into a car-sized patch of tall phalanx grass by the trail, then recognize the panting: It's Patricia, her fast, anxious breathing a familiar and usually happy sound. My heart swells knowing she's alive.

I stand and wave. "Patricia. It's Austin. Over here."

She freezes, takes two beats to trust what she hears and sees. Her hands are still bound, but not her feet or her mouth. She's wearing the same leather skirt and halter top she wore this morning in my condo.

She hurries to me, pulls me down with her beside the phalanx grass. "Mallory is right behind me," she whispers. "Can you get this off?" She pokes her hands at me. Duct tape binds her wrists. I find the edge with my fingernails and unpeel her. My lover sighs.

The closeness of her body arouses a tenderness I've only experienced before with Beth and Ryan. A hormonal cause for giving protection. Does that make any sense? I'm kind of new to this love thing. I think before, with the ex-wife Susan, what I thought was love was probably lust. You'd never understand now, looking like the old rhino she's become, but before she had two kids and went health food skinny, my ex-wife had a body I lost myself in. What I'm saying, these feelings I have for Patricia are new, akin to my instinctive attachment to my children.

A branch or a twig snaps close by. I know the sound belongs to Mallory. The time for battle has arrived—the reason I came, the reason a man is part of the team needed to raise children. I have to fight and protect this woman, my potential new family. I paw the ground for a suitable rock. There are dozens to choose from beside the trail. I whisper for Patricia to meet me at my Camry she'll find in the big lot, then point out how to cut across to the main trail by leaving through the phalanx grass.

She kisses my cheek and slips away.

The minute I came home today, the afternoon's events assumed dream-like qualities—Patricia's kidnapping, the chase to Sandy Hook—but the world now borders on fantasy, hallucination. The night wind and hissing surf become something larger in my head, a disturbing buzz that explodes in grand daydream, a highlight film of Patricia: *Flaming red hair catching light from the beach sun...freckles glowing in the candlelight of a dark restaurant...her fleshy breasts dancing above me.*

"Hey, asshole."

Mallory's voice blacks out my daydreaming. The back of my neck stiffens. The venom I hear in his voice wraps my fingers tightly around the rock, a fist-sized chunk of broken concrete. When I rise to face him, Mallory looms closer than I imagined. He's already coming at me from the back side of the phalanx grass. But near targets are bigger targets, so I throw, the rock flying perfectly off my fingertips—a strong, well-aimed fastball.

Mallory ducks my missile and keeps coming.

I figure Mallory expects me to back up in fear, so I charge low—dipping my shoulder and hurling my weight at his legs. I earn a double-scoop of fudge-ripple good fortune by surprising him. I take a punch on the back of the head, but my momentum remains, my shoulder landing hard against the leg Mallory planted weight on. Pain rips my collar bone when we make contact. But the telltale *pop* of snapping piano wire shudders through me. Pretty sure one of his knee ligaments broke.

Mallory and I both go down, him cursing as I roll away. Sand flies inside my mouth and nose. My shoulder burns with pain, but the ex-cop is down. Did he think I am completely helpless? That I'd freeze like some...stockbroker? The man failed to understand how the growling monsters we face each day—

"Put your hands behind your head."

Against the phalanx grass, Mallory sits with a drawn gun. I clasp my fingers behind my neck, elbows pointed out like bird wings. I feel like a pink, fuzzy hatchling, too.

"Where's the Willis woman?" Mallory says.

"I don't know. What do you guys want with her?"

Mallory points the weapon at my face, his lips spreading into a grin, the creep enjoying my fear. I'm a frozen snowman, waiting for the arrival of eternity, wondering what happened to my old T-ball coaching friend, the cop with a knack for teaching kids to hit. "Watch the ball hit the bat," Mallory would say. Over and over came the mantra—until they smacked it, which they always did, soon as they watched the ball hit the bat.

"Is this about the money, Jim? The ruby?" I ask. "Are you desperate since—you know, the hotel murder tape disappeared and you got fired?"

"Everything's about money," he says, "and nobody knows it better than you. I should blow your head off, bury you out here for the hawks to crap on. You prick."

He presses his weapon close, like he's going to shoot.

My mouth opens to say something—anything—when there's a swishing sound of moving air, followed by a *thump* and the simultaneous sight of Mallory's head jumping six inches sideways.

He topples onto the sandy dirt, blood oozing quickly from a gash behind his temple. A human shape walks out of the dark phalanx grass. It's Patricia holding a piece of driftwood.

Ms. Aguave Spikes and I hold hands as we run to the parking lot. I owe this woman for being brave, sticking around for the battle, but I can't stop worrying Mallory is right behind us. Maybe Vargas. How does he play into this? They mentioned his name. I have something everyone wants apparently, a redhead with important information.

I wait to ask questions until we're inside my Camry, the engine running, a way out of the parking lot in my high beams. "Do you know why Mallory brought you out there?"

"That old bird platform scares me, and Mallory knew it. He wanted me tell him and that man Rags what I knew about the ruby. And I think maybe Vargas was on his way...Mallory said he was coming."

"Do you know why?"

"Just that it was about the ruby," she says. "Rags or Mallory must have been the one who shot Vic, right? They had it. They told me the ruby was a fake. They asked me what I did with the real one, and what happened to the money that was inside."

"Rags overhead Vic making arrangements for delivery, no doubt. But I wonder what Mallory has to do with it."

"Mallory brought Vic the Las Vegas connection. He must have talked Rags into a cut."

The two of us ran on pure adrenaline minutes ago, shocked by the nights events. Now, in the darkness of the steady straight drive, my Camry purring, we're crashing like drug addicts. "I think it's risky going back to my condo or your apartment," I say. "How about a hotel?"

"Whatever you think." Patricia throws her head back, tries to breathe deeply. "Think I killed Mallory?"

"No, but I wish I'd checked. How about Rags? It sounded like someone threw him off the bird platform."

"Mallory and Rags started arguing, so I ran," she says. "Mallory must have pushed him off. I wonder if he has the ruby."

Mama Bones, Gianni and captive James Mallory are in Mama Bones' basement kitchen, Mama Bones kicking at the dirt floor with her shoe, her fingers tight around the stag-bone handle of her twelve-inch carving knife. Mallory is tied to a chair near the stacked barrels of olive oil.

"It was me, I'd start with his left forefinger," Gianni says. "Show him the pain and let him think for a while about life without his thumbs."

Mama Bones makes a face. "Oh, that's too mean for my old friend Jimmy Mallory. He's already hurt. Look at the side of his head, huh? I'm only gonna cut off his finger—if he refuses to talk. First we try my special tea. No use spending all that money on peyote and Bolivian bat testicles if you're not gonna use them."

She reaches for the Fed-Ex package.

EIGHTEEN

While Mama Bones waits for her truth potion to work on the ex-cop, she and Gianni play head-to-head poker at the table in her basement kitchen. None of that sissy Texas hold 'em stuff either. Five card stud. In forty minutes, Mama Bones wins more than a thousand dollars.

"How come you always know when I'm bluffing," Gianni says.

"You gotta tell, smarty pants."

"What is it?"

"I'm not gonna say. Not for nothing anyway. How about two thousand?"

"You're kidding?"

"A thousand?"

Gianni's head stops shaking when Mallory groans. Both her nephew and Mama Bones gaze carefully at their prisoner. Mallory's eyelids flutter like little bug wings. Sweat drips from his pink forehead.

Mama Bones pulls a chair close to mister hard-ass Mallory. The chair rakes the soft dirt floor. She wets her lips, drops her rear end on the seat and waves at Gianni. "Turn down the lights."

To further soothe her drugged and hog-tied subject, Mama Bones gently washes Mallory's forehead with a cool, damp cloth. She made a bowl of water and ice right after he drank his tea, so the water is good and chilly on Mallory's sweaty face. He groans with relief.

"Hello, my friend Jimmy Mallory," she says. "It's your fairy godmother."

He groans again. Probably having some weird distorted vision.

"Do I get a wish?" he says.

Or maybe not. This is very good, though. Mister tough guy here thinks he's in control of himself. Giving her lip. "Of course you get a wish," Mama Bones says. "That's what fairy godmothers are for, right? What would you like, huh?"

"How about untying my hands."

Ha. This is why fresh bat testicles are worth so much money. They have a calming effect on your victim's overall sense of well-being, and sometimes—like today—they make people think they are completely normal, unaffected by the potion. Mallory is going to tell Mama Bones everything she wants to know, all the time thinking he's not.

"Oh, that's a very good wish," Mama Bones says. "I'll be very happy to grant that one. Untie your hands. Sure, no problem. All you gotta do first is tell me what kind of business you were doing with my son Vittorio."

"Vittorio?"

"Vic. Vic Bonacelli. What were you doing for him?"

"I ran an errand," Mallory says. "Made arrangements."

"Arrangements?"

"Talked to some people for him. Sell something."

"Sell what? To who?"

"Vic had some good info—inside information about stocks. I told him I knew some people in Vegas who might pay for that kind of thing."

Mama Bones grins at Gianni. She knew Vic would not mix himself in her official family business, not without asking. She knew it had something to do with the redhead's information.

"How much did Vic sell it for?" Mama Bones asks.

"The deal I made him was a hundred fifty grand," Mallory says, "but it got switched up along the way somehow, Vic ended up taking a ruby instead."

"A ruby ring?"

"No, a stone. A pretty big one, too. Had a name."

Mama Bones takes her time, pours herself a glass of Gallo Bros. Paisano. "What were you doing out on Sandy Hook with that redhead tonight, huh?"

"Trying to find out if she knew the ruby was a fake."

"What?"

"A fake. Rags and I had the ruby checked out by a pro."

"Wait. How did you two get the ruby?"

"Rags shot Vic, took the briefcase. I followed him, got the drop—"

"Rags shot my Vittorio?"

"Pretty sure. I heard a gunshot, saw Rags come running out of Patricia's apartment with Vic's briefcase."

"You were there, too?" she says. "You see my nephew Gianni?"

"Sure. In that ragged Jeep."

"Okay, so Rags runs out with the case, then what?"

"I followed Rags home, got the drop on him later and cut myself in. I could have shot him, taken it all, so he agreed we'd sell it together, split the money, sixty-forty, me taking the lower share because all I wanted was what Vic promised me for introducing him to Las Vegas. He said he was going to stiff me. Maybe you'd like to make it up for him, you being my fairy godmother and all?"

"Make it up why? You got the ruby. Oh, no, that's right. It's a fake. So it sounds like you had more reason to shoot Vic than Rags."

"I'm not stupid enough to shoot your son, Mama Bones."

"You're stupid enough to cut yourself in on a fake ruby deal. Maybe the stone's real and you're lying to me."

"That's why Rags and I wanted Patricia out there on Sandy Hook. Find out what she knew about it."

"Why the tower?"

"She fell off the old one in high school," Mallory says. "One night during a wild party. She was always afraid of it afterward."

"You're kidding. You knew the redhead in high school?"

"Didn't everybody?"

"Okay, so how did Rags fall off the tower?"

"I pushed him."

"Why?"

"I wanted the ruby. Like you, I was thinking maybe Rags tricked me, set up the dealer we went to see—the guy who told us the rock was bogus."

"You just happened to think of this then, on the bird watching tower?"

"Yeah, because Rags kept bringing up Vargas, saying maybe Vargas gave Vic a phony ruby in the briefcase. I thought he was over-doing it, you know?"

"Sounds maybe true."

"Not if you know the people Vargas works for. They make a deal, it's a deal. Vargas wouldn't dare cheat their client."

"I know people like that, too," Mama Bones says. "In fact, I kinda *am* people like that."

"I know."

"So where is the ruby now," she says.

"In the trunk of my car."

This Irish ex-cop knows how to make Mama Bones smile. This is turning out to be a special day for Mama Bones. First the news from the hospital that Vic is out of serious danger and recovering. Now Mallory leads her right to the treasure someone stole from her son. Vic isn't dumb enough to pay for a fake ruby.

From a lonely pay phone, I make an anonymous call to the Branchtown police. Rags could be in need of medical attention. Mallory, too. But I don't do the right thing, step up and identify myself, tell the cops everything I know. I mention mayhem and injuries near the bird tower on Sandy Hook, leave it at that. Instinct tells me to talk first with Luis.

I walk to my car and Patricia, both of which I've parked a block from the phone booth, then navigate toward the center of Branchtown. It's barely nine o'clock when we park at Luis' Mexican Grill. The hotel can wait.

Luis Guerrero pours a draft beer for a customer as we walk inside. A heavily male crowd watches overtime football—the New York Giants versus the Dallas Cowboys. Takes me eight minutes to tell Luis the story of Sandy Hook, how Patricia and I ended up at his horseshoe bar. While listening, he offered Patricia and me something to drink. Now, he's down to business.

"Is it possible James Mallory is alive and followed you here?" Luis asks.

"I don't know if he's dead or alive," I say, "but he couldn't have followed us. He wasn't moving, and we would have seen the headlights of anybody who followed us out."

"And you are certain Santo Vargas—the man who attacked you at my wedding and at the hotel that night—was not there as well?"

"Positive," I say. "I didn't see him. Only heard Rags mention his name."

Luis walks away to pick up a short stack of bills from across the bar. Each step, every hand movement is flawless, his body repositioning itself with perfect efficiency. To me, he's like watching a wild animal perform. Beneath the quiet walk, you can see the athleticism, the natural savage.

"Where's the lady's room?" Patricia says.

I point. "Head toward the kitchen, but make a left down the hall before you get there."

Watching Patricia's hindquarters pitch and roll away from me, I wonder again at the lovely chemistry we had right from the start—that kiss at the wedding, the first day on the beach, our sexy bodies in my bed.

Luis returns. "I am about to close the restaurant—as soon as the football game is over. I think it would be wise if you and Patricia stayed with Solana and me tonight. There is an unused bedroom in our new house."

"I was thinking more like Mexico," I say.

"It will not solve our problem to run," Luis says. "Santo Vargas must be dealt with. He should have gone away after failing to hurt you on the night of the wedding, so he stays for a reason. I believe he and this Mallory must be working together, perhaps to acquire the ruby you mentioned. Or more likely to challenge me."

"Why does Vargas want to challenge you?"

"Come stay at my house tonight," Luis says. "We will make plans and Solana will tell you about Santo Vargas. It is more her story than mine."

This sounds interesting. Plus having Luis protect me sounds like a nifty idea, maybe what I've wanted since the day Vargas assaulted me after the wedding. Then again, I'd hoped to get lucky tonight, and who knows how agreeable Patricia will be to my advances under Luis and Solana's roof.

Speaking of Patricia. The sore place on my forehead itches, and I remember where Vargas attacked me. The bathroom.

"Luis!"

He catches on immediately when I mouth the name Patricia. He has to lift a flap on the bar and adjust a patron in his stool, but Luis still beats me to the hallway.

"She left you to use the rest room?" Luis says.

"Ten minutes ago. Something's wrong."

Luis calls to a passing waitress. "Estelle, *mi amiga*, come here, please."

His hands reach out to take her tray of food. "Please go into the ladies bathroom, *por favor*, and see if there is a woman with pointed, silver and black hair."

Luis stares at me while we wait. "Remain calm."

Estelle comes back and reports there is no sign of Patricia.

I search the parking lot while Luis checks every corner of the restaurant. *Nada.* I'm frightened that bastard Mallory somehow followed us and then grabbed her, but who knows, maybe Patricia ran out on me.

By the time we've given up searching and Luis is ready to have me follow him home, I've pretty much decided she took off on her own. My heart feels abandoned. But Luis believes the worst, that she has been kidnapped, and worse still, Luis believes Santo Vargas is behind it. He begins an early closing of the restaurant.

Mama Bones is in bed trying to sleep when the doorbell rings. She pulls on her bathrobe and lifts her new Sig Sauer semiautomatic from under the pillow. She checks the load and clicks off the safety on her way down the stairs.

At the front door, she listens. Like she figured, it's Gianni. He can't stand still and is always shifting his feet. She slips the semiautomatic into the pocket of her bathrobe, slides back the door's dead bolt. "I thought you were spending the night at your girlfriend's," she says. "What's the matter?"

"The ruby's definitely a fake," Gianni says. "Pure glass."

NINETEEN

I park across the street from Luis and Solana's two-bedroom bungalow on Kadrey Street, their home bright in the moonlight. Hundreds of these post-World War II homes exist on Kadrey, the main drag from Branchtown's river front to the Atlantic Ocean—four miles of tiny, wood-frame two bedrooms, all built between 1947 and 1955. The Guerrero edition is newly painted white with dark window trim, and sports a new composite tile roof. A knee-high, neatly cut evergreen hedge trims a healthy lawn. Luis bought the run-down property six months before the wedding and worked on the place every day since.

Jogging across the street, a nip on the breeze and a flash of weariness stiffen my gate. I slow to a walk. Cold weather is coming. Freezing rain, snow, and ice. No more going barefoot. Even after all the years I've been gone, I still miss those mild winters of southern California.

Luis greets me on his porch. He's changed out of his work clothes, wears a charcoal cotton sweatshirt and jeans. Same black Reeboks. Luis probably does everything with quiet determination, but there's something purposeful about his hand on my shoulder—military, or at least coach-like. I suspect major advice looms.

"I believe we must find Santo Vargas tonight," Luis says.

"Patricia probably ran away," I say. "We don't know anybody kidnapped her, let alone Vargas. It was Mallory who took her from my condo."

"Of course." Luis pushes on the door to his home, holds the varnished wood open for me. "Let us go inside. I think after talking to Solana, you might decide we cannot wait to find out. I will make telephone calls while my wife tells you her story."

I follow my friend into the sixty-five-year-old kitchen—as narrow as a sailing yacht's. Solana chops tomatoes on the tiled counter. Luis' bride wears a flowered blue apron over jeans, a white T-shirt and a smile like she knows I'm thinking it's an odd time for her to be playing chef. She's cooking at ten o'clock at night?

"Hello, Austin," Solana says. "How are your children?"

I will never repeat the story Solana tells me. Though it happened years ago, when she and Santo Vargas lived together in Las Vegas and admittedly used heroin, meth and other drugs, Vargas assaulted and abused Solana in ways so sick, so cruel, I cannot understand how she speaks of them, how she shares with me the details. Vargas swore Solana would always be his slave, and actually held her in chains prior to her escape.

When she's finished her tale, Luis comes back into the kitchen, leads me into the spare bedroom. There's a single bed, a three-drawer dresser and a desk piled with papers, all pushed against one wall. Even in these domestic surroundings, even in black jeans and the charcoal sweatshirt, the ancient warrior shines from inside Luis' black eyes. To protect friends and family, here is a man ready to lose centuries of civilization.

"Solana and I hope you will not share her past with others," Luis says.

"Of course, never." The Toltec warrior made his wife tell me her story for a reason. I ask him. "Are we going to kill Vargas?"

"I believe such an outcome is possible."

My butt rests on the neatly made double bed I was to have shared tonight with Patricia. The cover is embroidered with blue flowers in long rows. A painting of Jesus watches us from above the varnished oak dresser. "I have to ask you something, Luis. After what Vargas did to Solana, why haven't you killed him before?"

Luis' dark eyes simmer. "Solana did not deserve to be attacked in *any* manner, let alone the vicious way Vargas defiled her. Yet she chose to be with such a man, and remained after he became violent. These things happened before I knew her. I will not kill a man to satisfy my pride, or even Solana's."

"Why kill him now? We can't be sure he took Patricia."

"If he has not taken her, we will do nothing. Of course. But you told me Mallory was prepared to shoot you when Patricia hit him with the driftwood, and I cannot believe Vargas' name was mentioned without reason. You told me yourself Las Vegas is behind the insider trading, the ruby. Is not Santo Vargas their emissary? And I warn you that if Santo Vargas wants Patricia—or anything belonging to you—you and your family's lives are in danger, not only Patricia's."

"You think Vargas would hurt Ryan and Beth?"

Luis stares at me. "Do you think he would not? He almost killed you at the wedding and again later in the hotel. You know these men will do anything for money or to protect themselves. Did you not tell me your children's mother saw a black SUV parked near her home? Your troubles will not cease until this man Vargas has left."

After a light meal, Luis and I begin preparations for an assault on Santo Vargas. We start by dressing for a beach party and packing into my car. I have no clue why. I just do what I'm told. Luis ushers Solana into the back seat, then climbs into the shotgun seat beside me. "Park at twenty-two fourteen Atlantic Avenue," he says.

"The Atlantic off Ocean Ave?"

"*Si.* Go straight down Kadrey and make a left turn at the beach."

"In Jersey we say *shore.*"

He grunts.

I don't know where Luis is pointing us, nor what we will do there, except ultimately we are looking for Patricia Willis, and ready to battle Vargas if he forces a fight. Luis says first we must establish alibis and acquire at least one weapon. Personally, I have doubts, but Luis has convinced me my family and I are in mortal danger. After the story Solana told me, the thought of Vargas going after my children is more than I need to go along. I know I'm letting Luis influence me. But in the past, this has been a good thing.

In the rearview mirror, Solana's Aztec nose and rocky chin form a silhouette against the back window. When she leans forward, getting ready to speak, I see a pointed sharpness on her features I also expect to hear in her voice. Luis' new bride is not happy.

"This is foolish," she says.

Call me Swami. Her tone snaps Luis' head around.

"I would prefer you not speak of our plans tonight," Luis says.

His wife glares at him. The first of many such looks, I am sure. Get used to it, Luis. Ugly glares are a cornerstone of married life.

"You prefer my silence because you know I am right," she says.

In the quiet that follows, I again consider tonight's mission. For me, it's difficult to justify taking another human life. Morally, there *isn't* any way to justify it. But tonight I *will* try to kill Vargas if events force me. If not to physically protect his children, what more natural purpose could a man have in this world?

Except for a star or two peeking through the overcast, the only light on the beach comes from a raging happy campfire. Red and orange flames bounce six feet high. Black shadows of men and women dart and dance across the fire, singing, drinking, laughing.

The music is Latin salsa, and loud enough to keep up with the steady crash of surf. The temperature's cold, a breeze off the ocean. I smell salt, seaweed, and a whiff of beer from the party. In jackets, hoodies and jeans, this generally young and Latin crowd looks like they're warm enough to go all night.

At the edge of the party, before we join in, Luis touches my shoulder. "Say nothing," he says. "Remain at my side and do as I do. We are going for a swim."

I stare into his eyes. Luis stares back—and doesn't like something he sees.

"Are you all right with what we have planned tonight?" he says. "Perhaps killing a man?"

I nod, aware Solana's watching me, too. The sand chills my feet as if I were barefoot. Luis is concerned, and that unnerves me.

"Say this to me," Luis says. "Tell me what you are willing to do."

My gaze finds a shimmer of light on the ocean. That the sea is eternal is hardly an original thought. Almost everyone feels it. The scientists say this ocean is where all life comes from. I feel it now. Strongly.

"Austin?"

"If I get the chance, I will cut Vargas' throat with a broken bottle," I say.

Luis nods, then hands me two extra-large plastic baggies. "Take off your clothes."

TWENTY

The cold black sea hugs me close against her bosom, sucking heat from my body and strength from my will. For the first time since Luis and I waded into the Atlantic, I don't think I'm going to make it. The colored strip of lights—Branchtown's boardwalk—is much too far away. Numb and soul-weary, I am falling asleep. My fingers and toes are senseless, my arms and legs swim with the guidance of memory, not feeling.

"Luis."

My friend's head bobs above the next wave, as if he'd expected trouble. Luis reaches across an ocean of rising water and grips my shirt, twisting the material into a ball and lifting. I pop up buoyant again, like a hollow beach ball.

"We are almost to the shore," he says. "The swells are pushing us in now. You must relax and kick."

Luis wraps my left arm around his neck and helps carry my weight as we emerge from the surf. I need help, but the heat of his body begins to revive me right away. My feet press against the wet sand with increased feeling. My knees turn from rubber to plastic. I'll be all right in a minute.

We've landed in a sandy cove beneath a beachfront mansion, one I recognize—a blocky but ornate replica of a French chateau that sits a quarter mile north of the salsa beach party. This is the biggest house on Ocean Avenue in Branchtown, right at the end of Kadrey Street. The New York owners close the place every summer on Labor Day.

My legs and spirit warm up. By the time we cross the sand and reach the chateau's driveway, where a friend of Luis' waits with towels, warm black clothes and a package of other goodies, I no longer need assistance.

"I borrowed for you a dark Chevy Impala," the friend says. "And I have switched the license plates."

Luis is already sliding into a pair of dry black sweat pants. Me, I want that towel. The beads of water on my skin feel like crushed ice. All this for an alibi, the right to tell police we never left the beach party?

Warm air rushes against my face through the stolen Impala's open side window. Broad Street in Branchtown is empty—a string of colored bulbs, shop windows, street lamps, and unoccupied traffic intersections, green and red lights. My eyes blink with the memory of how far away the city looked from a quarter-mile offshore.

I glance at Luis. "So I guess you know where Vargas lives?"

"He sleeps on a construction site. If he has Patricia, she could be there as well."

Luis turns right on Main and parks half a block down, across the street from a large excavation. One dozen two-story condos are going up, prices starting at nine hundred thousand. The pit they're digging will be underground parking. A billboard tells all, even that the construction company is headquartered in Las Vegas, Nevada.

"How did you find him?" I say.

"Solana knows the Russian men Vargas works for in Las Vegas. The same men are responsible for the construction of this new building."

With his fist, Luis breaks the Impala's interior overhead light. The northeast horizon thinks about turning blue-gray. A few birds chirp outside, but the big morning chorus hasn't started yet. Any minute.

Luis hands me a short-barrel revolver that was in that bag of other goodies on the beach. A Smith & Wesson. Thirty-eight caliber, snub-nose, I think they call these puppies. "If Vargas is here, it is likely that he and I will fight," Luis says. "Use this revolver only if he kills me."

Now there's an unpleasant thought. Luis' death. I glance at the Smith & Wesson. Not my weapon of choice, of course, but in some situations, the Carr gift of gab becomes inoperable. Vargas rushing at me with a switchblade the size of Brooklyn might fall into that category.

"You got it," I say. "I'll do it."

I've already turned this night over to Luis. I'm not going to argue how he plans the battle. The king of Stockbroker Special-Ops is still just a stockbroker. Luis is Luis. I follow him across the street, the two of us racing like mice into the black shadow of the construction site's billboard. An orange, two-story crane, with its long, giraffe-like neck, blocks the dirt road down into the excavation. The crane's tank-tread base prevents the site's perimeter chain link fence from completely closing.

Luis and I scurry from the billboard shadow to crouch by the construction crane's huge treads, then squeeze through the gap in the fence. My shoes skip-slide on rocks as we descend the steep dirt and gravel roadway into the excavation. Beside me, a network of thick rebar holds back the earth, a reinforced wall that grows quickly into a two-story barrier against the dirt. Near the floor of the excavation, the ancient smell of wet earth punches my nose, and I flinch at something over my shoulder. It's the crane, hanging above us—a giant steel dinosaur.

On the flat bottom of the construction hole, Luis stops and puts his hand on my chest. Ahead, in the back-left corner of the square excavation, two glowing windows of an aluminum trailer stare at us—big yellow eyes studying their prey. Thick cables run to and from the trailer like twisting snakes. An early train for New York whistles its arrival at Branchtown station.

Luis approaches the trailer. "Vargas!"

He makes the man's name sound like a species of lizard. Loud enough for Vargas to hear, if he's inside this trailer. But probably not shrill enough to wake any neighbors. The closest people are not only above the rim of the underground construction site, they're also a block away.

No response from the trailer.

The discordant train whistle blows again, this time announcing NJ Transit's lonely departure. My head is buzzing with bad vibes.

"Come outside and face me, *puerco*," Luis says.

A thump sways the silver trailer, left to right. Some internal mass moves heavily to the aluminum door. My pulse thuds like a boom box as I glance at the rim of the excavation to check for witnesses. There is no one else on site.

The trailer door bangs open. Vargas jumps down, his switchblade open and ready.

Luis crouches, his knife out of his pocket in a blur.

The two men circle each other, slow dancing around an invisible perimeter. Not a word between them. Aren't they going to call each other more names? *Puerco* hardly seems enough to cause all this trouble. It's as if the bell rang for round one—like the two of them do this every day in a Disney World wild west show.

The size difference shocks me. I knew Vargas was bigger, huskier, but his shoulders and legs, the chest especially, make this side-by-side comparison an overmatch.

"We came for Patricia Willis, not a fight," I say. "Is she inside?"

"If Luis cuts me badly enough, you can have a look," Vargas says.

Vargas darts forward. It's only a feint, and he comes right back to that unseen perimeter. But not before Luis reacts, shifting his feet and weight defensively.

"So be it," Luis says. "The women you have abused cry for justice."

Vargas grunts. "The women cry for my cock. Including your bride Solana."

Luis' face turns to marble.

My hand clutches the revolver in my pocket.

TWENTY-ONE

Luis explained to me once about knife fights. The big secret to winning? Don't use your knife. Sounds crazy, I know, but Luis says it's the hand *not* holding the knife that usually wins the contest. Because a knife can kill, inexperienced fighters tend to only watch the blade. They're not keeping close track of their opponent's empty fist.

Both Luis and Vargas seem aware of the big secret. Both hold their knives across the left palm, saving the stronger right hand for a punch. They advance opposite each other in a slow circle, dueling crabs in a march around that invisible perimeter, claws extended. As he sidesteps, Vargas' bare feet make little sucking sounds in the mud. The dank smell of wet earth clings to my throat. The blue-black sky grows a shade lighter.

Vargas holds his switchblade like he's cutting bread, so the knife makes his reach longer. He's ready to stab and slash with it, or punch with his right hand. Luis holds his switchblade like an ice pick. His reach is shorter, but if Luis stabs downward, he can muster his entire body weight behind the thrust.

The windows on Vargas' trailer put the life-and-death contest in a single rectangular spotlight. I half expect a crowd to chatter and catcall from behind the wall of dirt and darkness that surrounds us. Automobile tires swish by on Broad Street a block away. The gun in my grip steels my nerves.

Vargas feigns left, then charges Luis' right side, slashing twice as he lunges. The second and more athletic of the two knife thrusts strikes Luis' left arm. Worse, Vargas anticipates Luis' reaction. The man with purple eyes and tattoos on his neck drops into a crouch, ducks under Luis' counterattack, and gives himself a clean, open stab at Luis' chest.

I gasp. Vargas' thrust flies toward my friend.

Luis snap-twists in a blur and catches Vargas' blade with his already wounded left arm, dancing backward as he absorbs the second blow. The material of Luis' black sweatshirt hangs shredded from the lacerated arm, dark liquid already spilling from the wrist onto his left hand and the switchblade.

I pull the revolver out of my pocket. I'm not going to let Luis die, not without trying to prevent it. Luis shifts the blade to his right hand and changes to a tip-forward grip like Vargas. His weight settles back on his heels. Luis might be in trouble, getting defensive like this. He staggers, and I know I'm right.

I aim the revolver at Vargas' back. "Put down the knife."

Vargas twists so that Luis and myself are at opposite sides of his peripheral vision. From between us, he can watch us both. When he glances directly at me, had a good look at me and my weapon, he spits.

Guess Santo Vargas doesn't think much of stockbrokers. I decide to compensate by talking tough. Besides, he's so close I probably can't miss with the revolver. "I know you watched my children's home," I say. "I *will* shoot if you don't drop the knife. I only want this fight to be over."

There's no hesitation, no signal for me to read prior to his lunge. In the split second it takes me to see and understand the man is coming after me, Vargas has already covered half the distance between us. The tip of his switchblade streaks like a missile—straight toward my throat. The man is fast.

The weight of the revolver doubles in my hand. My hair stands up. But I squeeze the trigger.

Maybe because we're below ground level and the earthen walls so flat, the explosion stuns me like a punch, the noise attacking my chest, not only the ears—as if I'd been forced against a hard surface. In the blue dreamy flash accompanying the big boom, I glimpse Vargas taking a bullet high on the right chest, his upper body spinning from the force. His forward momentum continues, but I sidestep the now-wounded charge.

Vargas stumbles and collapses onto the damp soil.

I run to Luis. My friend is on one knee, breathing through his mouth. I pry away his fingers, open the sweatshirt above his wound. I'm looking at a bad gash. Blood flows steadily. I knew Luis was in trouble, but his condition might be worse than I thought—Vargas might have nicked an artery near the bone. Bastard knows how to use that knife.

Ripping off the sleeve of Luis' sweatshirt, I produce a tourniquet. I cinch the cloth tight under Luis' armpit and directly over the gaping, heavily bleeding cut. I know my adrenaline is pumping. I can hear myself panting. But I'm focused on the knot—tying a good one so Luis won't bleed to death.

"Check inside for Patricia," Luis whispers. "Then we must leave."

My gunshot no longer echoes in the giant dirt pit, but the air tastes of gun powder. I check the condition of Mr. Purple Eyes before I enter his trailer. Vargas has assumed the position of a wounded slug—curled into a ball on the damp ground. Not a twitch. Maybe the bullet in the chest killed him.

Inside Vargas' trailer, I discover the man lives like a slug, too. The place reeks with dirty clothes, pizza boxes, fungus-growing remnants of a donut, and soda cans. A steel desk with stacked mail, a new Apple desktop computer and a wire rack with a handful of manila file folders clutters a corner nightstand. A refrigerator, shower stall and a single day bed mess up the rest of his space.

But no Patricia. I even check the shower stall and under the bed before ducking back outside. Luis has staggered to the bottom of the trailer steps. His jaw hangs open, my friend still breathing through his mouth. Gasping, really. I wonder how much blood he's lost.

"She's not in there," I say. "This was all for nothing."

Luis shakes his head, the movement slushy, un-Luis like. He's not himself. Hurt. "I cannot understand how," he says. "My eyes left him only for the briefest of moments—"

"Him? What are you talking about?"

"Santo Vargas..."

I look over Luis' shoulder, then around him. *Hell*, no.

"...Santo Vargas is gone," Luis says.

Vargas' trailer was tiny. Even checking the shower and under the day bed, I was inside maybe thirty seconds. How could Vargas disappear in so short a time? Right under Luis' nose. It's impossible.

"Where did he go?" I say.

"I do not understand," Luis says.

I jump down. The excavation is dark, but there is clearly no Vargas. No one at all. Could Vargas have run all the way up the sloped equipment road, completely left this construction site? I don't see how. Not with a bullet inside him.

"You didn't hear or see anything?" I say.

Luis shakes his head. Wobbles might be a better term. I need to get him to a hospital emergency room. Where is Vargas? Behind the aluminum home on wheels, out of my sight, is...what? I still have the revolver. Shouldn't I search on the far side of this trailer, and in the shadows by those two, five-foot tall generators? Maybe behind those piles of aggregate rock. Vargas could be hiding.

No. Luis needs a doctor. And we came for Patricia.

I check Luis' wound. My tourniquet slowed the bleeding dramatically, but Luis could die if an artery's been nicked. I snuggle close and wrap his good arm around my shoulder, catch some of his weight as we hike back up the dirt equipment road. It's slow going, one heavy, careful step at a time. Kind of like Luis walked me out of the ocean an hour ago.

"You have witnessed a rare thing, *amigo*," Luis whispers. There's a tiny smile on his lips. "Not since the age of eleven have I lost a fight."

"You weren't doing well, true, but I stopped it before you actually lost."

He grunts. "*Muchos gracias.*"

My muscles are flowing with power juice. Who knew fear could make you stronger. Or is this feeling the result of shooting someone like Vargas? When we reach the top, Luis and I are a tight, awkward fit between the crane and the fence, but we manage, and at the car I almost drop Luis before stuffing him in the Impala's passenger seat.

"Remind me never to dance with you," he says. "You are clumsy."

Ha. The guy gets in a fight, he starts throwing around quips like Arnold Schwarzenegger.

The quickest route to Navasquan Hospital takes us past the U.S. Army's closed Fort Monmouth, soon to be developed into parks, condos, and boat slips. The two-story geodesic dome that houses the Army's big radar glows bright orange, a reflection of the rising sun. It's dawn on the Jersey Shore.

"Your shot must have missed," Luis says.

It's a good thing Luis is talking. Glad he's conscious. But he happens to be full of crap. "I didn't miss. I saw the shot hit his shoulder. Spun him around like a doll."

"Perhaps he wore a bulletproof vest," Luis says.

I nod. "That might work."

Luis says, "Where are you taking us?"

"I'm headed for the hospital emergency room."

"I must agree. There is no longer a need to complete our alibi by returning to the beach party. Call Solana and suggest she meet us at the hospital."

Across the next intersection, I pull to the curb and open my cell phone. "Let me ask you something, Luis. If Vargas survived, what do you think he'll do? I mean, will he come after us?"

"Santo Vargas' actions are difficult to anticipate."

There's no answer on Luis' house phone. His wife could be in the shower, or even in her garden at this hour, the sun up. But Luis worries when I tell him.

TWENTY-TWO

Solana hasn't answered the phone all morning, so Luis wants to roll as soon as the emergency room doctor is finished with his glue, staple gun, a transfusion and questions about the nature of Luis' injury. We're there five hours, but the doctor—a short, cautious guy with thick glasses—wants Luis to spend another twenty-four of them in a bed resting. When no one's looking, we mount a jailbreak.

We dump our stolen car across the street at the Branchtown train station, catch a cab to my car that's parked near the beach, drive to Luis' house. The morning sky broods with gray-black clouds, and the Guerrero bungalow on Kadrey Street rests in the shade of a neighbor's century-old spruce. But even from the sidewalk we can see Luis' front door is ajar.

Can't believe I have any adrenaline left, but there's enough to stay close to Luis as he runs to the porch and pushes inside. Overturned furniture greets us in the cozy living room. Spilled drawers and broken dishes litter the kitchen floor. My stomach flops imagining what Luis' bride could look like if Vargas came here to hurt her.

"Solana!" Luis' voice has a nasty edge.

He pushes me toward the kitchen clutter as he hustles left into the bedroom. Luis' wounded condition worries me. The disheveled state of the house scares me. And the way Vargas skipped out on my gunshot in the chest or shoulder gives me the freaking creeps. Before I go off on my own into the kitchen, I pull out the revolver.

Smith & Wesson can walk point.

There's little light in the tiny 1940s kitchen. Outside one of the room's two small windows, a thick and happy Japanese black pine blocks most of the morning sun. The sugary smell of ripe bananas makes me wish I was slicing fruit on my breakfast cereal instead of holding a gun. The world is upside-down when stockbrokers are armed.

I hold still to listen. A garbage truck or delivery van rumbles past on the street outside. There is always something moving in Branchtown. Luis bumps or shifts something in another part of the house. He's searching.

"Solana?" Luis' voice is muffled but I can still hear that edge.

The kitchen counter is made of tiny one-inch tiles, maybe the original installation. A stainless steel sink and new, double-paned windows above the faucets all face the rear of Luis' property. Coffee-cup size clay pots of cactus and succulents adorn the window frame over the sink.

A reminder of my California past—a red-spine barrel cactus—draws me closer to the window, and I reach for the pot and a better picture of the backyard. As the clay pot cools my fingertips, motion in the vegetable garden draws my eye. I squint to focus on a splash of bright red bobbing among orange pumpkins.

I shout. "Solana's in the back."

I hurry to the rear porch so she can see me. By the look of her jeans, garden gloves, and raggedy-ass flannel shirt, Solana's been picking and carving pumpkins all morning. The red bandana around her head, Apache style, is covered with wet pumpkin seeds.

Luis stumbles onto the porch as she arrives, shielding her eyes from the sunlight breaking between the clouds.

"You do not answer the telephone?" Luis says.

"What happened to your arm?" she asks.

"A small cut. It is nothing. Why did you not answer the telephone?"

Solana props her hands on her hips. "I've been in the garden since breakfast, Senor Detective."

Luis frowns. "You have not been inside? You do not know that our furniture has been overturned, our dishes and lamps broken?"

Solana's forehead crinkles. "What?"

"The front door was open when we arrived," Luis says. "Every room has been searched. You heard nothing?"

"*Nada,*" she says.

Solana examines Luis' wounded shoulder. "What have you done that brings such violence to our home, my husband?"

In my kitchen the next morning, while I rinse and fill the drip machine, pull my grinder down from the cupboard and wrestle with the Colombian Supremo coffee beans until my pot is brewing, the same old whirlwind of questions spins through my addled brain: Where's Patricia? Am I headed to jail for insider trading? What else did Rags hear with that secret microphone in Vic's office? Was it Rags or Mallory who shot Mr. Vic and stole his ruby?

"Morning, Daddy," Beth says.

She's in the living room—somewhere—and though instantly recognizable, my daughter's voice gives me a jolt. I thought I was alone, plus I have that loaded Smith & Wesson under my pillow. "Good morning to you, too," I say. "You let yourself in last night to sleep on my couch?"

"I came by really late," she says. "I didn't want to wake you, so I fell asleep out here watching TV."

My daughter's purple-tipped fingers appear on the back of the sofa, then her hands as she hauls herself up into a kneeling position, showing me her ink-stained hoodie and blue jeans.

"Are you coming back to live with me?" I say.

"Not for good. But...you know...when I need to."

"You're always welcome, Toots, but we have to let your mom know. Get a schedule."

"Oh, she knows I'm here," Beth says. "She and Bob called last night from Atlantic City, said they were stuck and I should stay here."

Would have been nice if Susan and Bob the Dentist told *me.* I almost say something, but shut up because I don't want my daughter to feel she's imposing. Beth takes things so negatively right now.

"Mind if I nap here on the couch another hour or so?" she asks. "There's no school today."

"Wouldn't you be more comfortable in the guest bed?"

"Not really."

When I'm satisfied my coffee machine is working properly and my first morning cup is in fact on its way, I scoot to the sofa and give Beth a kiss on the head. She's not thrilled, but tolerant. "Whatever you want," I say. "Go ahead, sleep right there. I'll take the newspaper back to my bedroom."

"Thanks." She curls up like a puppy and closes her eyes.

First thing I do in my bedroom is unload the pistol, hide the empty gun in a sports jacket, the five remaining bullets in a black wingtip shoe I haven't worn in five years. Then I read the paper. When I'm done browsing the sports section, the coffee should be ready, so I tiptoe down the hall into the living area.

Beth's invisible and silent, asleep on the couch. I slide by the bar stools at the counter, turn into the kitchen and freeze dead, heart pounding like a schoolboy in love. A familiar figure sits at the kitchen table watching me. Santo Vargas. Wish I had that loaded revolver now, although I'm not sure what good it would do me. So far Vargas seems immune to .38 caliber ammunition.

"What do you want?" I say. "I don't know where the ruby is. I don't know where Patricia is."

"I want only to talk. For instance, the red gemstone is a spinel, not a ruby."

"Huh?" Though I have never heard the word before, my confusion is due only in part to his use of the term spinel. A bigger reason is that I just remembered my daughter Beth sleeps twenty feet away.

The skull tattoo on Vargas' neck winks at me. "The coffee smells *muy bien*," he says. "Pour two cups. We will sit and discuss gemstones—and your future."

If something happens to my daughter...I try swallowing the lump in my throat. No dice. The mound of dirt will remain stuck in my esophagus until Vargas and Beth no longer occupy the same space. I tell myself to keep breathing.

In the kitchen, I concentrate on filling two mugs with coffee. I manage to start thinking again by the time I serve Vargas. He sits at the four-foot, oak dinette table by a window that looks onto a common courtyard. Not many leaves left on our deciduous trees. I choose the chair next to the window, the seat beside him, not because I'm feeling friendly, but to face me, Vargas must twist his vision away from the living room.

Vargas takes a pull on his coffee. "Excellent," he says. "We both like our coffee strong."

Vargas sports a convincing, relaxed manner. His hands and lips have a light hold on the red mug, his shoulders visibly settling as the coffee hits his stomach. The poor guy needed his morning cup. Wonder how he got inside my home and how long he's been sitting here. He sure isn't worried I might have my gun handy, who might be lurking in the bedroom or stretched out on the living room sofa. Could he have already checked?

"I need to ask you a question," Vargas says. "Perhaps more than one. If you answer honestly, I will leave, and no harm will come to you or your daughter asleep on the sofa. Can you tell me only the truth?"

TWENTY-THREE

My heart stops when Vargas says *daughter.* If he knows Beth's here, on the sofa, he could have already hurt her.

"Yes, of course I will tell you the truth," I say. "Whatever you want to know. Anything. Please don't hurt my daughter."

Santo Vargas studies my face for two beats. "She is fine. Asleep. Now please, if you will, recall for me who told you about *La Gran Hechizo.*"

My pulse restarts. "*La Gran Hechizo* is what? The ruby?"

"*Si.* In English, the big spell or big mojo. Once a legendary gemstone on the crown of an Indonesian prince, the red stone—thought to be a ruby—was discovered to be a spinel."

"What's the difference?"

"Spinels are a different chemical composition, softer, and a separate form of crystal. They are beautiful but not nearly as valuable. The prince sold it."

"Patricia Willis told me about the gem," I say. "She called it a ruby, said it was a payoff to Mr. Vic for an insider stock tip—someone in Vegas."

"The Big Mojo was part of an agreement I had with Senor Bonacelli," Vargas says. "But how did Patricia Willis know I came from Las Vegas?"

"Vic told her. Patricia's the one who gave *him* the stock tip, so she was always scheduled to get part of his payoff."

"Ah, this makes much sense," Vargas says. He sips his coffee. "When did this conversation between you and Patricia Willis occur?"

"A week ago—right after Vic was shot."

For a brute with tattoos on his neck, the guy handles a mug with grace. Maybe I'm just surprised he doesn't burp.

"Did Patricia Willis know the names of the people from Las Vegas?" he asks.

"No. But she said they were Russian."

Vargas' purple eyes squint at me. "Are you certain she mentioned no names?"

"Positive. And you know it's true because you didn't tell Vic the names, only that they were Russian. Patricia only could have heard that from Vic."

He stares at me longer than two beats this time. My salesman's intuition tells me I'm scoring points. I'm so frightened for my daughter I'm having trouble analyzing—I'm plowing forward on instinct.

"Did Patricia see who shot Senor Bonacelli?" he asks.

"She *said* she didn't. The man stood in a half-open doorway, a hat over his eyes."

My daughter's disheveled hair peeks above the sofa. From my perspective, Beth can be seen over Vargas' left shoulder. I fight to keep her moving image in my peripheral vision and not give her away.

"So Patricia told you this man both shot Senor Bonacelli and took his briefcase containing cash and the Big Mojo?" Vargas asks.

"She knew about the gemstone, I'm not sure about the cash. She told me she threw the briefcase at the guy's head to keep him from shooting her."

My sixteen-year-old daughter slides to the fireplace. I choke, warning Vargas, when Beth picks up my fireplace poker.

Vargas spins, sees her and without leaving his chair, motions for my daughter to put the poker back where she found it. This bastard is calm, even grinning at me when Beth complies with her intended instrument of attack.

"Do you think she might have the ruby?" Vargas asks.

"My daughter?"

He laughs. "No. Patricia Willis."

"Sure. Why not? She keeps disappearing. I can't say I totally trust her."

"And yet you are in love?"

My mouth opens but seconds pass before words come. "I guess so. Sometimes it's hard to tell."

"Ha. This is true, is it not? Like the spinel and the ruby, sometimes a thing is only a weak imitation. But then I think also that love is a good thing, Senor Carr. In whatever form. Real or fake. Love is what brought me here to New Jersey. The business I had could have been done by others. But I wished to see Solana again."

"You love Solana?"

"Perhaps. Or I feel guilty over things I have done in the past. As you and I agree, it can be impossible to discern the real from the imitation."

Vargas gulps his remaining coffee and stands. "Goodnight, Senor Carr. Let us hope my business with you is finished."

"Why aren't you calling the police?" Beth's crying. Her words sound like bleats, each one a tug on her daddy's heart. "That man threatened your life," she says.

"Forget the police," I say. "You heard him. He's done with us."

Now that Vargas is gone, the poor thing is scared to death. One minute Beth's prepared to knock Vargas' head off with a poker, ninja girl style, the next she's whining like a normal sixteen-year-old. Took some serious moxie to grab that poker, to imagine sneaking up behind Vargas to hit him. She could have gotten us both killed, but still. That is *some* daughter I squired.

I'm still seated at the kitchen dinette with my mug of coffee. The ceramic container warms my hands and fingers. Funny, but Vargas' visit has me feeling toasty all over. Wasn't he just a swell guy. Makes me worry.

"Did you steal the ruby?" Beth asks. "Is that why you can't call the police?"

"No. Of course not." I'm in a strange mood, one I can't define. "Vargas was here because I tried to kill him, Toots. I shot him with Luis' gun. I can't call the cops about *this* without them finding out about *that*, see?"

"You shot him? Holy shit, Daddy. You *are* in serious trouble."

"Watch your Language. Have some coffee."

No use running down my list of problems for Beth, but lying is bad, too. She's too big, too smart, and too much of a potential problem to kiss off. Her mother could take me to court and bury me with this information. My only chance is to take Beth into my confidence, tell my daughter the truth. Kids act like they don't give a rat's butt about anything, but in my experience, they worry about everything.

When she's poured herself a mug, added the cream and sweetener like her dad, Beth says, "So whose ruby is it really?"

"Honey, please. You don't need to understand everything. In fact, the less you know about these details, the better."

"Don't you trust me?"

"Of course I trust you. But I'm involved in a federal investigation over a stock market tip."

"Is the tip connected to the ruby?"

"Maybe. Listen to me. I'm being investigated by the U.S. District Attorney for New York and the U.S. Securities and Exchange Commission. Any day, a man or woman with a badge could hand you a court paper *forcing* you to answer their questions under oath. When did your father meet this man? What did your father say? Who did he talk to on the telephone? If you lie, or even if they *think* you're lying, you're going to jail."

My daughter's eyes grow larger by half.

"I do not want you faced with that situation," I say.

"I think Vargas is a hit man for the Russians," she says.

"Stop." I had the same feeling.

"Okay," she says. "I need to jump in the shower anyway."

"Where are you going?"

"Unofficial water polo practice this morning."

"Water polo? That's a rough sport."

"It's physical, but fun," she says. "And I'm good at it."

"You're a championship swimmer. Of course you're good at it. When's the first match I can watch?"

She's already on her way to the bathroom. "I'll let you know."

My daughter stops in the hallway, comes back. Damn if she isn't wearing a full-boat Carr grin.

"Can I ask you something?" she says.

"Sure, Toots. What?"

"Are you in really love with that Patricia woman?"

Oh, my. My mind rambles through implications and ramifications. It's my sixteen-year-old child I am talking to here. What is it one needs to say about love?

"No lectures, Daddy, okay? Just say yes or no. Do you think you are in love with that lady?"

"I don't know. Maybe."

"How does *anyone* know if they're in love?"

I drink coffee but it doesn't help. "Love takes time. You have to test it. In a way it's like the discussion I had with Vargas—there are lots of red gems in this world. Some are glass, some spinels, and a few are real rubies—one of the hardest substances known. And like rubies, real love can stand all tests."

I'm pretty proud of this analogy. I'm sure the comparison sucks and days from now I will realize the shortcomings, but now the red glass story feels very fitting—educational even.

She waves goodbye. "I knew I'd get a lecture."

While Beth showers I sit at my dinette table and watch airplanes streak across the sky through my kitchen window. A steady line of bumblebees, leaving the hive. Today, the bumblebees head out every two minutes.

Funny what Beth said about Vargas being a hit man for the Russians. Odd that he admitted to being in town to payoff to Vic. Why would he tell me that? I'll have to run that by my attorney Mr. Zimmer this afternoon when I see him. Zimmer was asking about Las Vegas, did I know anybody there. Now I do.

TWENTY-FOUR

My tall, stern, and go-for-the-throat German lawyer addresses the golf ball like the hack he is, weight on his heels, head bouncing, the brand new Titleist orb aligned off his front toe. If Randall Zimmer, Esquire gets lucky and actually *hits* the white dimpled sphere, I guarantee this first drive slices dead right.

"Watch me," Zimmer says.

I nod. You don't talk on the tee when someone's getting ready to hit, although I suppose it's a gray area if you're the one teeing off *and* talking. When someone new to golf like Mr. Z asks me to play with them, hand out pointers, I spend most of the day teaching etiquette.

"Any last minute tips?" Zimmer says.

"You should be visualizing the shot, not talking, Mr. Z. But like I said, you'd play better if you moved the ball back in your stance."

"Yeah, the pro says that, too. But I'm comfortable like this. Both of you also say I should be comfortable."

"All righty then. Just relax and keep your head down."

Mr. Z jerks into his backswing then chops at the golf ball like he's trying to kill a snake. His first tee shot scampers across the grass tee box like a white mouse and disappears into the locust tree woods forty yards out on the right.

"What did I do wrong?" Zimmer says.

"Everything."

I'm still explaining about balance and keeping your head still as we finish the fifth hole. Mr. Z's ready to try a new stance, but two foursomes already wait to hit on the next hole, a par three. After a twenty second consultation, Mr. Z and I decide to pack it in for a beer.

We zip in our electric cart to the halfway house, grab a couple of Sam Adams and two hot dogs, settle down in the park-like setting. Mr. Z and I choose a black, iron-mesh table under a Cinzano umbrella. The little patio is surrounded by a waist-high wrought-iron fence.

"I had another reason for getting you out here today," Zimmer says. "I wanted to talk to you about your case, but outside the office."

I wash down a bite of hot dog. "What's up?"

"Your story is a tough one to sell," Zimmer says. "A man currently in a coma signed onto your account and bought the stock without your knowledge."

I shrug. "It's the truth. Mr. Vic and I are the only people who know the master password."

"Fine, but we have to convince the U.S. District Attorney and the Securities & Exchange Commission. We have no evidence Vic Bonacelli broke into your account. In fact, there is only your word it could have happened. Plus, it strains credibility to claim you weren't aware of the purchase until after the merger when everyone saw you meet before the merger date with Patricia Willis."

I finish my Sam Adams. Would it strain my credibility to order another? How about if I stood up, yelled four-letter words rapid fire and at full volume, cursing my semi-conscious junior partner, Mr. Vic. "So in summary," I say, "I'm screwed when we go to New York next week?"

Mr. Z sips his beer. "Let's say fifty-fifty you'll keep ownership of the firm and your principal and sales licenses. The illegal trading profit in your account will have to be returned, and there is the distinct possibility of a fine."

What started out as a lovely stroll in the park, a breath of fresh air, has evolved into disaster. No wonder Mr. Z wanted to meet outside his office. His partners didn't want a bloody mess if I killed myself. Darn. I knew there was a chance I could lose my licenses, but I always figured Mr. Z would pull something out of his four-hundred-dollar-an-hour hat. I sigh. Looks like I could easily end up selling Toyotas.

"It gets worse," Mr. Z says. "If you tell this story under oath, and we can't prove it...if the District Attorney believes you're lying...well, do you remember Martha Stewart?"

"You mean I could go to jail for telling the truth?"

Mr. Z's nod can only be called grim, and in a flash I understand the *real* reason he brought me to the golf course. He didn't want to wear his suit and tie when we talk. My straight-laced German member of the bar needs help stepping outside the lines.

"Are you suggesting I change my story?" I say.

Mr. Z's fingers tap against the glass beer bottle. "I'm an officer of the court. I cannot and will not present any evidence I know to be false."

"Of course."

"But...perhaps we need to consider going another way with this."

I spread my hands. "Like what?"

Mr. Z takes a long pull on his beer. Besides the change of clothes, the natural setting, maybe he also needs alcoholic encouragement to tell me what's on his mind. I definitely want to hear what my man has to say. Kind of exciting to think of the big German breaking rules.

"Speaking theoretically," I say.

He makes a show of sighing. "Let me put it this way. If another attorney were to look at this case, I believe he or she might comment, 'The District Attorney seems so focused on Las Vegas, it's too bad your client didn't admit his wrongdoing. He might have been able to save his license.'"

"But I'm innocent. I did not act on that tip. I did not buy that stock."

"Did you say tip?" Zimmer says.

At the halfway house concession window, two crew-cut, thirty-something golfers snap their heads in our direction. Tip? Everybody wants inside information.

I lower my voice. "We went over this. I was in Vic's office when Patricia told the story about—"

"Wait," Mr. Z says. "Before you tell me exactly what Patricia said—seems to me you were a little vague before, and my earlier notes are lost—I want you to go home and think about that word."

"What word?"

"Tip. I'm thinking how Ms. Willis described the information to you is very important—that is, was it really presented to you as fact? Or perhaps Ms. Willis was regurgitating a story she'd heard elsewhere from an unknown source."

"She said it came from her—"

"Stop. Don't say another word. I want you to think hard about what was said that day. Was it inside information or just another hot tip?"

Okay, I get it.

Early next morning I drop off Beth at water polo practice and come back to my condo for a morning of coffee and the news. I'm old fashioned, still like to check out the local rag for the police blotter and other Branchtown stories. I'm reading an hour or so when the telephone rings. It's Beth.

"Was that guy's name Vargas or Vargo?" she says.

"Why? What are you doing? I thought you had water polo prac—"

"Daddy, please. I did, but I've got ninety seconds. I want to look him up on the internet in computer class later."

"Do *not* get involved with this, Beth. I told you that."

"How am I involved? I'll Google his name, see where it takes me, e-mail you what I find, that's all. You know I'm good. I could turn up something. I want to be an asset, not a liability."

Oops. That's a line from one of my parent-child lectures. "All right," I say. "His name is Vargas. Santo Vargas. V-A-R G-A-S."

Late that afternoon at work, she calls again.

"Daddy, it's Beth. Did you know Santo Vargas is the manager of a Branchtown construction project that's like six blocks from your office?"

"As a matter of fact, I did know that. That's where I shot him. Now listen, Toots, I want you to drop this. No more Santo Vargas."

"Mike knows one of the cement guys on the project," Beth says. "He's going to show us around. Maybe I can peek inside Vargas' office."

What? My pulse jumps. "You stay away from there! Do you hear me? I don't want you anywhere near that man."

"Vargas is not in town," Beth says. "That's why Mike's friend says he can take us down inside the excavation. We're just waiting—"

"No, no, no! You mean you're already at that construction site? Oh, my God, Beth. What were you thinking?"

"I want to help you. Mike does, too. He brought me after school. Maybe Vargas has something to hide, something that will make him leave you alone."

"You need to leave that construction site right now. Do you hear me?"

"Daddy."

"I mean it. Right now. I'm going to have a heart attack worrying if you don't leave."

"I want to help."

"I know. But please. Do you want me to have a stroke?"

"You said heart attack."

"Are you going to leave that construction site?"

"All right. We'll go."

"Promise?"

"I promise. I'll tell Mike."

"So where are you going? You headed home or to my condo?"

"Probably the library. I have homework to research. Then Mom and the dentist's tonight."

I was going to say, why not go home and Google what you need, but it occurs to me the public library might be a safer place than her house, or certainly my condo.

"Okay," I say, "Maybe I'll see you tomorrow. But I expect you to keep your word, right? You and Mike are going to the library now?"

"I promise. See you soon."

I walk back to my Camry. The fact that I am going to drive by Vargas' construction site does not mean I don't trust my daughter. What it does mean is her actions—or inaction in this case—are too important. Daddy can't afford to have doubts.

In particular, I search for a motorcycle Beth mentioned once as belonging to Mike, but since I don't know for sure, I make two passes around the excavation block and check every parked car. Nothing. Looks like Beth kept her word.

TWENTY-FIVE

Down in her dirt floor basement kitchen, at the desktop computer, showing Gianni a new piece of her business, Mama Bones double clicks on Year-To-Date. No good. Her share of the bingo games is still running seven percent under last year. Maybe if she offered the priest fifty-two percent instead of fifty, Father Malamud could be talked into adding an extra night. If they played a full stack of cards, revenue should rise at least—

Standing behind her, Gianni paws her shoulder. "What's that?"

"What's what?" Mama Bones hates being distracted.

"That noise. Sounded like the front door. You know that big click the old thing makes when it closes or you work the handle."

"Go check. You're making me nervous. And put the fake ruby away somewhere while you're at it. I left it out on the sideboard last night in the blue Tiffany box. I'm gonna give that hunk of glass to my sister Albertina for Christmas."

Gianni struts from the room. She listens to his feet on the stairs, and then marching down the hallway and across her living room. Jogging now from the sideboard to the door, heavy shoes pounding. That's funny. He takes another four or five minutes before he comes back, too.

Standing in the doorway, he says, "The fake ruby's gone. The front door was still open."

Mama Bones clicks the computer mouse to make a month-by-month colored graph of the bingo take. "Somebody got big *cojones* breaking in here."

"Crazy, or a drug jones. And all they got was the Tiffany box with the glass—must have heard me coming up the stairs and ran."

Mama Bones clicks to write Father Malamud an email. "Yes, it's-a strange. But who really cares about a piece of glass, huh?"

Gianni says, "But doesn't it make you wonder who took it? I mean, sure, it's probably some crackhead from another neighborhood, doesn't know who he's stealing from. But what if it wasn't? What if the thief came here looking for—and thinking they would find—the *real* ruby?"

Mama Bones frowns. Her gaze loses focus on the computer graph. Interesting point Gianni makes there. Who doesn't know that thing is a fake? Or wants it to be real...

"Call the boys, quick," she says.

While Gianni pushes little buttons on his fancy black cell phone, Mama Bones drags down on the file, clicks on save and shuts down the program. She is smelling action tonight. Big time action. She stands up and stretches.

Gianni's phone gets a ring back in seconds from his crew-wide email. He listens, then says, "Vinnie at the end of the street—the guy who took you to the airport last year—he's sitting on his front porch, says Patricia Willis raced by minutes ago, turned left onto Willow. She's driving a blue Ford Mustang."

Mama Bones grabs her purse. "Get your gun and the car keys."

For the exercise, mental break and to carefully consider what Mexican delicacy I will eat upon my arrival, I walk to Luis' Mexican Grill for dinner. It's a crisp fall evening, the sky washing pink and pale orange as the sun sinks. On my way, I text Beth to make sure she's at the library.

My cell phone vibrates a few minutes later while I'm walking across Luis' gravel parking lot. When I see it's not Beth I come close to not answering. My phone doesn't even recognize the incoming number. But I say hello anyway.

"It's me," Patricia says. "Where are you?"

"Patricia! Are you all right?"

"I'm fine," she says. "Where are you?"

"I'm walking into Luis' Mexican Grill for dinner."

"Are you alone?"

"Yup. Want to join me?" My phone beeps from an incoming message.

"See you in five," Patricia says.

"Wait. Is everything okay? The way you disappeared—"

The loud honking of Canada Geese headed south over Luis' lot confuses me a second—kind of wish I was going to Mexico, too—but I realize Patricia has already shut off. I can't believe this woman. She's nuts. I don't hear from her for days, then she calls out of nowhere, teases me into buying her dinner. Like we spent last night together.

I hurry under Luis' canopy to avoid what I expect to be plentiful geese droppings. Each line in the flying V-formation of Canadas is a quarter-mile long. Checking the phone, I see there's a text back from Beth saying she's at the library studying, as promised. Reassured for no good reason—above all, Beth is a teenager and, according to her mother, capable of lying to me—I walk inside Luis' searching for two empty stools at *mi amigo's* bar. Funny, but my feelings for Patricia are not as strong as they were a few days ago. Some of that craziness evaporated while I was—and still am—distracted by my daughter's safety.

A buzz of conversation and the warm smell of fresh corn tortillas steer me toward a group of open stools near the top of the horseshoe bar, directly under Luis' most prized sombreros. I sit beneath an official Mexican Rodeo Association *charro*, and Patricia—if she really shows up—will dine to my right, under a black and white embroidered mariachi.

Glad to see Luis' left arm in a sling. He wasn't supposed to go back to work, but immobilizing the wounded limb is some concession to the healing process. With his right hand wielding a rectangular butcher's blade the size of a guillotine, however, he still works his job, currently hacking limes into green juicy quarters.

"There has been no sign of Vargas," Luis says. *Whack, whack.*

"Yes there has," I say. "He showed up at my condo this morning while Beth was there."

Luis rests his knife. "You and your daughter are unharmed?"

"Vargas was rather pleasant, actually. Barely threatened my life. I had to answer questions about Patricia, Mr. Vic and his stock market information, plus what little I know about that red ruby. Turns out it's really a spinel. That's—"

"Santo Vargas did not ask about Solana or myself?"

"No. He said he hopes his business with us is finished."

"Hopes?" Luis shrugs, picks up the cleaver, and resumes chopping limes. The first whack seems particularly aggressive. He says, "I am surprised Vargas did not kill you."

Haven't decided yet if I should mention what Vargas said about his feelings for Solana. I lift a menu from between bottles of hot sauce and the chrome napkin holder, glance at Luis' one-page list of daily specials. I made up my mind for chili Colorado on the way over, but the chili verde chicken special sounds awesome. Goat cheese infused tortillas.

A warm hand touches my shoulder. "Hi, Austin," Patricia says. "This spot is exactly where I left you."

Patricia sports red hair again, wearing jeans and a satin shiny blue top, the hair piled on top with teardrop sapphire earrings to match the blouse. I swear the bounce and curve of the jewels match the shape and sway of her hips. I cannot help but reach for her waist.

"You *left* me?" I say. "More like you ditched me. Why didn't you say you wanted to go? I thought you'd been kidnapped."

She touches my cheek. "Sorry, sweet talker. It was one of those spur of the moment, gosh I'm scared things. I had to run and hide."

"Why didn't you call?"

"I got tied up with—problems. That crazy mother of Vic's is after me."

"Mama Bones? Why?"

"She blames me for Vic getting shot, I guess."

I lean in close and kiss her cheek. She smells like a blue gardenia. I'm angry she ran out on me last time, curious why she didn't call. She had to know I'd worry. What was she up to? But when Patricia buries her lips in my neck, her tongue wet and hot, I forgive her. In fact, the craziness I thought might have evaporated surges once again. If you know what I mean.

Behind his bar, Luis directly faces Patricia. "You were rude to leave so abruptly the other night."

The redhead stops kissing my neck.

Luis points to his arm sling. "We went to much trouble looking for you."

"I apologize, Luis. I didn't think—"

"Clearly," he says. "Can I get you something to drink?"

"Oh." Patricia glances at me, takes a breath. "Just water, please, Luis. Thank you. My stomach feels a little—"

Patricia's husky voice trails off as Luis lifts his gaze. He stares above our shoulders, his gaze focused on the entrance to his restaurant. The way his eyes narrow snaps my head around. Who would worry Luis?

Santo Vargas.

TWENTY-SIX

There's a moment when Vargas' entrance matches the saloon showdown scene in one of those black and white cowboy melodramas from the middle of last century, and I am reminded once again how much Branchtown resembles my image of the old wild west. Not the guns and horses. It's the attitude: Like what's going on now—how conversations in the barroom stop and all eyes swing to the new stranger. Hey, I could be wrong, but seems to me like everybody in Jersey is ready to fight.

My image is shattered when Vargas cracks a thin smile our way. By the time Vargas saunters to my side and flattens both of his hands on the counter, his mouth of mirth is a solid grin, and the majority of Luis' patrons have drifted back to their enchiladas. I have to wonder what Vargas is so happy about.

Behind the bar in his arm-sling, Luis sidesteps to stand face-to-face with Vargas and those smiling purple eyes. Luis is most definitely *not* smiling, and by leaning forward aggressively, the owner of Luis' Mexican Grill clearly wants to make the confrontation nose-to-nose. One-handed, Luis wants to fight.

"You dare come here?" Luis says. "After searching my home? Breaking things?"

Vargas shakes his head. "I did no such thing. You are mistaken. For me, the trouble between us is over. I know your bride Solana will never be mine again. She loves only you."

Luis stares unblinking, speechless. I'm a bit shocked myself. The sharp *clink* of a fork or spoon hitting dishware sparkles against the background hum. This is still all about Solana?

"I came to your successful restaurant to tell you this," Vargas says, "but also to finish my business with *La Gran Hechizo*—or the Big Mojo."

"You spoke with my wife?" Luis says.

Guess Luis doesn't care about rubies, the Big Mojo in particular. I sure am curious, and so is Patricia. The redhead hasn't taken a breath since Vargas mentioned the jewel.

"Yes, I spoke with Solana," Vargas says. "Only this afternoon, and only over the telephone. It was wonderful that Solana finally agreed to speak with me. What she told me was not so pleasing, but certainly what I needed to hear. She made me understand her feelings, both about you and...her past."

Not a muscle moves on Luis' face.

"You are a lucky man, Luis Guerrero," Vargas says. "Solana is the reason I arranged to come to New Jersey. I could have easily sent another. But I hoped an apology, perhaps seeing me again and the gift of precious jewel would make her...take a new path."

Luis is ready to bite him in the neck. "Yet despite such a reasonable purpose, you injured my friend and tried to kill him by burning his hotel room? You threatened his children by watching his home."

Vargas' head wags no. "I was angry when I first arrived—Solana refused to talk with me before going ahead with the wedding. I sought to provoke you through your friend, encourage a fight, to prove myself the better man. Childish? *Si.* I did these things. But I never spied on any woman, your home or this man's family."

"Do you pretend your actions have been reasonable?" Luis says.

"No, I do not. And I would already be gone from this place but for my desire to complete a bargain."

"What bargain?" Luis says.

"Senor Bonacelli and I made an arrangement before he was shot." Vargas wears a black leather jacket cut like a Brooks Brothers blazer. He reaches for his inside breast pocket, making both myself and Luis twitch. But instead of a gun or a switchblade, Vargas withdraws a wallet-size blue Tiffany box. "I must deliver something before I return to Nevada."

Patricia gasps.

Vargas smiles at her, then lifts the Tiffany box lid to show us what's inside—a blood red gemstone roughly the size of an unshelled walnut. "I brought this jewel from Las Vegas to offer Solana," Vargas says. "But when she refused to speak with me, or postpone her marriage, I sold *La Gran Hechizo* to Senor Bonacelli."

"And yet here it is, still in your possession," Luis says. The owner of Luis' Mexican Grill is yet to be assuaged by Vargas' apparently honest revelations.

"By agreement with Senor Bonacelli, I kept *La Gran Hechizo* and left with him a glass replica," Vargas says. "A thirty-day, risk free trial, he called it."

"Sounds like Mr. Vic." I touch the Tiffany box, look at Patricia. "Does this look like the stone Vic showed you, the one in the jewelers briefcase?"

Patricia shivers like a mouse ran over her shoe, then reaches in her purse. I'm not the only guy watching who sucks air when she pulls out a blue Tiffany box exactly the shape and size of Vargas'. She places the box on the bar, takes off the lid. Oh, my. Now we have two Big Mojos shining the color of dark red wine, catching light from Luis' overheads and dazzling us with rose-tinted sparkles.

Vargas pushes his box and gem to a spot directly in front of Patricia. "Here you are, Senora Willis." He reaches for hers. "I will take back my glass one, *por favor*."

"Wait a minute," she says.

"Forgive me, Senora," Vargas says. "Senor Bonacelli is awake and told me over the telephone I should give *La Gran Hechizo* to you. I assumed he had mentioned this to you as well."

"How do I know *yours* isn't the fake?" Patricia says.

Vargas stares at Patricia. Luis and the redhead focus on the man with the tattooed neck. My eyes won't leave the red gems. I can't believe there are two.

"The ruby was my commission for information I gave Vic," the redhead says. "I want to make sure I get the right one."

"The gem is a spinel," Vargas says.

"Whatever," Patricia says. "The question is, how do I know you really talked to Vic, that this one is the real Big Mojo instead of the one I have?"

"Call Senor Bonacelli yourself," Vargas says. "He awoke from his coma late this afternoon. He spoke briefly with his wife and also with two Branchtown Police Detectives, I am told, a conversation which occurred in the presence of my informant. Here is his room's telephone number."

Vargas hands Patricia a slip of paper with penciled numbers. She finds her cell phone and starts poking. I don't like my Patricia is so hot to own the Big Mojo, Mr. Vic's expensive present. The Big Mojo is no *farewell* gift.

"Did Mr. Vic tell the police who shot him?" I ask.

"No," Vargas says. "He told the police he cannot remember the shooting."

Five or six business types—sports jacket or suit, shirts with collars and ties—noisily enter the dining room from the back of the restaurant. It's a walking Rotary Club meeting, storming Luis' Mexican Grill through the kitchen, the whole crew probably half-baked from beers elsewhere. Besides raucous laughter, the young business types bring along cooking smells from the kitchen, particularly cilantro and roast pork.

Patricia is having trouble getting Vic on the phone. She talks to someone in an over-pleasant voice. A young couple bounce through the restaurant's main entrance, and while I noticed their arrival from the corner of my eye, I now stare straight at them with what I hope is utter shock, fear and disbelief. Making a beeline for yours truly are my daughter Beth and boyfriend Mike. They are dying to tell me something.

Vargas twists, wants to see what I'm looking at, the shift putting big wrinkles in his black leather sport coat. "Your daughter," he says.

"My one and only." I wish Vargas didn't have so much information about my family.

Mike and Beth arrive bar-side. "What's going on?" she says.

"Too much to explain," I say. "Hang on."

"Vargas doesn't really manage that construction site," Beth says. "He has no experience. He must be in town for—"

"Okay," Patricia says. "Vic says I should swap my Big Mojo for yours."

"Think I'll take them both," a new voice says.

We all rotate our heads like a well-coached drill team. That's me, Vargas, Beth, Mike, Luis and Patricia, all twisting as one. We should have uniforms. Behind the Rotary Club businessmen, the new speaker limps out where we can see him. It's my old sales manager, Rags in shirt, tie and crutch, a disheveled tan suit with no left leg to accommodate an above-the-knee fiberglass cast. He's wearing blue sneakers. His hair sticks skyward in clumps. The whole package is a little scary, if you ask me, although definitely not as frightening as the semiautomatic in Rags' hand.

Luis and Vargas act at the same instant, Luis throwing a switchblade he's pulled from nowhere, and Vargas charging Rags directly, a blur of muscled shoulder and death's head tattoo. Vargas' hands are outstretched, reaching for the muzzle of Rags' semiautomatic.

Luis' knife misses. Fire from Rags' pistol stands up Vargas like a fence post.

I'm done watching. I throw myself at Beth and cover her with as much of my body and arms as I can press flat against her. A second gunshot from Rags' pistol drops Vargas to the barroom floor, and tightens the grip on my daughter. Being as gentle as I can, I lower my weight, tugging Beth to the restaurant floor, huddling us against the legs of a bar stool. I blanket her, with Mike helping me.

Silence becomes frightening. What's happening? Where is that bastard? I raise my head a few inches. Someone steps on my neck to scoop up the jewels. Rags.

My screwy former sales manager wrenches me off Beth by pointing the gun at her head. "Get up and lead me out the back door," Rags says. "Try to run, I'll kill your daughter."

"You, too, Luis." Rags backs someone off with the gun.

I scramble to my feet and wave Luis away. I'm so scared Beth will be hurt. I'm bordering on hysteria. Rags steers me around the bar, toward the kitchen, and I can't do anything but what he tells me. Especially once he lets go of Beth.

Luis won't fire his shotgun because of me and the crowd. This is it. Rags has me, my worst enemy. He hauls me through the cooking area where two assistants I met at Luis' wedding stare as we parade through. Both are fascinated with the gun resting against my head. Wire baskets of onions and peppers hang from the high ceiling.

Outside the back screen door, Rags drags me toward his old green Jaguar. It's no coincidence that one of the dents on his hood perfectly fits my butt.

"Give me your cell phone," he says.

"What do you want with me?"

"We're going to make cookies," he says.

"Cookies?"

I hand him what he wants. He tosses my cell in Luis's green trash bin.

"Trust me. You'll really get into it."

TWENTY-SEVEN

Driving Rags' old Jaguar, with Rags, his broken leg and the semiautomatic riding in back, my brain is worse than scattered. I'm seeing, hearing and thinking about my world in clipped bursts of semi-awareness. Like being drunk. I'm holding together on a single fact: At least Beth is safe.

"Head for your condo," Rags says.

"What for?"

"We're switching to your car."

My world is not right, and I have to do some serious internal dialoguing, talk myself back into a place where the things and people around make sense. Straighten it all out by separating the crazy whole into odd pieces I can understand.

Rags told me at Luis' a few weeks ago he wanted Carr Securities back, that he'd regain control one way or another. But the trigger happy psychopath ruined any chance, or any kind of normal life, shooting Santo Vargas with a restaurant full of witnesses. Something changed, or Rags isn't thinking anymore. Hell, Rags never did think much. I've been out-noodling Tom Ragsdale since the day he walked into the old Shore Securities. I've always known his plan before he did. Hope that still holds.

"The bug in Vic's office was pure genius," I say. "And the recordings must have turned up a lot of exciting information you didn't expect."

Praise always works on Rags, although it might take a while. This is not the same old Rags, the one a friend Walter and I used to torture with practical jokes. Gee, come to think of it, I could be partially responsible for Rags' mental problems, even the drug abuse. I'd sure like to think so.

"You must have heard Patricia's stock tip on that bug?" I say. "Why didn't you just score big on the inside info yourself? Or have you sent a copy of the tape to the U.S.

Attorney, trying get me and Vic tossed from the securities business?"

Rags doesn't want to talk it over yet. But he's *almost* ready. By staring straight ahead, ignoring me, Rags actually encourages me to proceed. For knowledge of human behavior, being a stockbroker for nearly a decade—we are essentially telephone salesmen—easily tops a degree in psychology.

"When did you decide to steal Vic's payoff from Vegas?" I say.

The skin beside Rags' left eye flickers. "Shore was supposed to be mine," he says. "Mr. Vic said so, at me and Carmela's wedding. The company *would* be mine today if it wasn't for you cheating Walter and me out of our stock."

An unbelievable take on past events. "When I bought your stock, *no* one wanted it," I say. "Business was crashing. The company was charged with co-mingling client funds."

"You told me and Walter all the clients were leaving. But you knew business was actually picking up."

Nonsense. Like any good salesman, I merely exaggerated the benefits and downplayed the risks of our transaction. I'd better change the subject. "Have you seen Mallory lately? I hear he's missing."

"Shut up and drive."

"Sure, okay. Did you try to kill Mr. Vic because he opposed you and Carmela reconciling, or because you wanted Carr Securities—or both? Was it always about the ruby? Seems like you want that gemstone pretty bad."

Rags sniffs. "That piece of crap rock is what screwed everything up. There was supposed to be money in that suitcase."

Mama Bones is going to catch a cold, for sure. Wet hair, the air outside cold as snow, and her head and neck stuck in this draft from Gianni's full-of-cracks old Jeep. Noisy as a tank inside here, too. And smelly. Probably it's the same World War II Jeep General George Patton crashed and got killed in.

"Try the heater again," she says.

"It's broken, Mama Bones. Honest."

The wind whistles against her ears and her hair. Mama Bones tugs on the stuck window crank one a more time. It won't budge. Gianni's Jeep has a one-inch hole up there between the glass and the rag top. If she catches a cold, maybe the hospital won't let her visit Vittorio tomorrow.

"We should-a taken a taxi," she says.

"Right," Gianni says. "Always good to have a stranger along for the big finish, now we finally have the real ruby and Vic's shooter in sight."

"I'm gonna get sick," she says.

"Sorry, the Escalade's in the shop."

Mama Bones shrugs. Maybe Gianni is right. This is no time to complain. So what if she catches a cold or the flu, has to wait a day or two to see her boy in the hospital. She got lucky tonight, she and Gianni following Patricia to Luis' Mexican, Gianni spotting Tommy Ragsdale's Jaguar. That rotten drug-addict, ex-grandson-in-law of hers, Tommy Ragsdale, he surprises Mama Bones. She always knew he was nuts, but a cold-blooded killer? Shooting her son, Vic, and then shooting that guy Santa Claus Vargas. Twice. When Gianni told her that's what he saw through the restaurant window, she first couldn't believe him. Who knew stockbrokers could be killers, huh?

"Looks like they're headed to Carr's condo," Gianni says.

Rags pokes me from behind with his semiautomatic, encouraging me to push his Jaguar through semi-yellow lights, fleeing pedestrians, and clearly visible stop signs. I'm going too fast as we bounce in my condo driveway. Halfway through a turn in the building's rear parking lot, a white Mercedes flashes red tail lights too late and backs into us.

I get my foot to the brake, send the Jag into a short screech, but there's not enough time or space. *Bam.* We smack the Mercedes hard enough to wrinkle the Jag's hood, but the airbags fail. Lucky for me.

"Crap," Rags says.

I've never liked Mercedes. They just ooze status or something. If I had to initiate an auto wreck, take my choice of all the cars I could smash, I'd pick a Mercedes. I unfasten my seat belt and pop the driver door. Maybe I'll make a run for my freedom.

"Don't get out," Rags says. "Keep going. Back us up and go around."

Our little accident did not dislodge my former sales manager's grip on that gun. It's aimed between my ears for emphasis. I re-close my door, swing around the wounded Mercedes.

"Hey, asshole!"

It's the owner of the Mercedes, shouting as I drive by, a big guy who wears nice blue suits. I see him around the condo building lately, usually with a pretty young woman. The guy's over six-foot, two hundred pounds, with black hair and a California tan. He's far enough away to ignore for now. My car is parked at the other end of the lot, a half a block away.

I gun the motor and chew up the distance, pull the Jag alongside my Camry. Rags motions with the gun to wait while he opens the door. The car port's concrete and brick back wall rises only three-quarters of the way to the roof. Through the gap, stars twinkle in a dark blue sky. The salty sweet aroma of cooking soy sauce drifts my way from the Hunan Wok restaurant next door.

Feet slapping on concrete turn my head.

"I'm talking to you!" The man in the blue suit moves fast. He must have sprinted all the way here. "You hit my car," he says. "It's messed up. You're not supposed to drive away from an accident."

I nod toward my armed companion, Rags, his crutch and the semiautomatic currently struggling out on the other side of the Jag. "This guy has a gun, so I'm doing exactly what he tells me to, okay? Worry about your car damage later."

"Who has a gun?" Mr. Mercedes says.

"Me," Rags says.

My ex-sales manager shows him, too, the semiautomatic rising above the Jag's roof, the black muzzle aligning with Mr. Mercedes' neck. Odd, but the big guy doesn't look frightened.

In fact, he shows Rags what's already in *his* hand—a leather case with a gold badge and U.S. identification.

"Put down that weapon," Mr. Mercedes says. "I'm a Federal officer."

Rags limps around the back with his crutch, stands six feet away and aims the semiautomatic at the Federal officer's chest. "Look in my eyes," Rags says. "Do you see who's talking to you? I shot two people in the last half hour. Want to make it three?"

The cop puts away his badge, raises his hands.

Rags points at me with his weapon. "Find his gun."

I reach inside the cop's coat. I've been dying to check the brand of his suit anyway. Nice blue suits are the mainstay of every stockbroker's wardrobe. Kind of like the young single woman's little black dress.

"My weapon's in my car," the cop says.

He's wearing a Canali. I should have known. Nothing looks as good to my eye. I explore every nook and cranny of the three or four thousand dollar suit, but find no weapon or holster. He does harbor stainless steel handcuffs hooked on his belt.

"Check his ankles," Rags says.

I lift his trouser legs, exposing socks of pure silk but no spare weapon.

Rags waves his pistol. "Get in the Camry, officer. Lie face down on the back floor and put your hands behind you. Carr, help him put his cuffs on."

"Why are we taking *my* car?" I ask.

TWENTY-EIGHT

I'm flat on my back, tied up, staring through my Camry's window at the starry night and mostly nude trees. The leaves are all gone up here in northern Jersey, dead, and sure as shootin' I could be next. My taped hands went numb beneath me five minutes ago, and with my head stuffed under the arm rest like a lost toy, now my neck is losing feeling.

My cushion is softer, but I think the dark-haired Federal officer has it better on the floor, even though Rags has the seat way back to drive with his cast. The cop owns a bunch more head room. He and I are both gagged. His breathing sounds ragged.

I twist my hips, trying to ease the pressure on my neck. My face rubs the arm rest to cure an itch, and a corner of the duct tape over my mouth peels loose. I rub again, and again, and enough tape peels loose from my mouth, I can press the unattached corner against the upholstery. The tape sticks well to the fabric, and slowly I peel my mouth off the gag.

Did Rags really think he could shut me up? I own this bozo.

"Tell me, Rags. How did Mallory talk his way into your action?"

"Crap."

"Did it hurt much when he threw you off the bird watching tower and broke your leg?" I ask.

Rags snaps his head over the seat to check me, no doubt making sure the tape on my wrists and ankles is still in position. That's what I'd be checking if the guy I just gagged started talking.

"Your nose is bleeding," he says.

"Drop me at the hospital."

The cop on the floor hums and mumbles behind the silver tape across his mouth. I roll my shoulder and slide my hip so that my arms dangle over the edge of the seat. If the Federal officer can move at all, if he gets his head and mouth up high enough...

"What's going on back there?" Rags says.

My fingertips touch the cop's forehead, then his nose, and finally his taped mouth. I grip the tape edge hard with my nails. His lips peel away from my hands and the tape.

"Thanks," he says.

"Crap," Rags says.

"It's Patricia Willis' actions I am interested in," the cop says. "Not anyone named Rags or Mallory. We believe Ms. Willis may have stolen inside information from her brother's locked desk at a family dinner."

"Who the hell is we?" Rags says.

"My name is Arnold Casey. I'm an Investigator for the U.S. District Attorney in New York."

Oops.

"So that parking-lot collision was no accident?" Rags says.

"Yes and no," Arnold says. "We've been watching Carr for weeks."

Gee, how bad can the news get? Makes me almost glad Rags is going to kill me. Almost. I can't believe that an hour ago I was enjoying a tequila, watching and listening to Vargas explain rubies, spinels and the last three mysterious weeks of my life. Things seemed pretty good. Resolved. And now this—

"You don't want to do anything drastic, Mr. Ragsdale," Arnold the cop says. "When I don't check in minutes from now, every asshole in Jersey with a gun and badge will be looking for us."

Now that *is* good news.

"In a few minutes," Rags says, "you and that dickwad will have disappeared from the planet."

Cold air whistles against her neck glands. Mama Bones' back and shoulders are stiff as wood. She grabs onto the Jeep's stuck window crank one more time.

Mama Bones knows what those Alcoholics Anonymous people mean when they talk about the craziness of doing the same thing, over and ever, expecting a different result. But maybe this time, at least with the window, she'll get lucky. It could happen.

Nope. Ha. Those AA people who meet in St. Theresa's basement every Wednesday night, drink all that coffee, they're right this time, too. Still no dice with the window.

"Sorry about the window and the heater," Gianni says. "But Rags is pulling off the Parkway. That should help. Exit 142, like you predicted."

"Okay, that's-a good."

Not only will the wind drop, maybe Mama Bones will get something entertaining to look at while they follow Tommy Ragsdale, Austin Carr, and whoever the other big guy is they picked up in the condo parking lot.

"You were right," Gianni says. "He's headed for work. That left turn we just made puts us on the same street as Ragsdale's bakery. "

"How many men you got coming?" Mama Bones says.

"Lots."

The sign reads Aunt Lena's Homemade Cookies Corporation, Piscataway, New Jersey. I catch glimpses of a three-story stucco wall, lines of Aunt Lena's purple delivery trucks, and a block-long loading dock with twenty stalls, all covered by one tin roof. Rags slides my Camry under the half-acre metal cover and shuts off the engine. Arnold Casey's labored breathing fills the back seat with a soundtrack of distress.

Pain stabs my neck when Rags drags me out of the back seat. My butt and lower back land on asphalt that smells like old engine oil. An airliner landing at Newark-Liberty hisses through the night clouds as Rags slices the tape around my feet with a box cutter. "Stand up."

My hands are still taped behind my back, so I roll onto my knees and stagger to my feet. While I watch, Rags slides on new clothes—a green, one-piece coverall, the white and red logo of Aunt Lena's Cookies stitched on the breast pocket. *Tommy* in red script above the logo.

"How nice."

Rags shoves me, and I stumble closer to the double steel-door rear entrance. On my right is the row of twenty delivery trucks. Behind Aunt Lena's massive cookie truck fleet, an empty lot stretches to the black horizon with waist-high, brown weeds. Room for further expansion of Lena's cookie empire.

Rags turns his back on me to grab Arnold's feet. On a whim, I break into a run. It's impulsive, not the product of careful thought. My animal spirit guide must be a horse, plus I used to sprint the one-hundred-yard dash back in high school. I mean, I can run. My best time was fourteen seconds, sure, but Coach said my form was excellent.

With my hands tied, resulting in an off-kilter running motion, my normally good form does not play. Not only am I slow, but I'm unable to catch myself nor cushion my fall when I trip ten yards away. Rags' grabs my shirt, bounces my head off the asphalt. A hive of wasps screams inside my skull.

Me stumbling, Rags nudging my back with the pistol, we troop back to my Camry. I've taken so much physical abuse the last two years, I should invest in new, more defensive means of transportation. Maybe an F-15 with a full complement of Hellfire missiles.

"Crap," Rags says.

It takes me two seconds to figure out why Rags is miffed. Arnold Casey is no longer in my Camry. Rags' head jerks this way and that. Where could Arnold have gone? His feet were taped, his wrists in handcuffs. The way he was breathing, I can't believe he got himself off the Camry's plush rear carpet.

Rags pulls my arm. "Let's go."

His semiautomatic again directing traffic, Rags hustles me to double steel doors that serve as Aunt Lena's employee entrance. Two spotlights beam down on the cement steps from a bracket above the doors. Rags keys the lock.

Inside, he flips a switch and eight long fluorescent overheads pop on. We're in a dressing room and break area. Steel lockers cover two walls. Three round tables with folding chairs swallow half the floor space. Candy, soft drink, and snack vending machines guard the far wall.

"We taking a coffee break?" I say.

"Shut up."

Rags punches numbers on a wall-mounted, black keypad. The lockers across from me are dirty and old, like the kind I had in high school. Round, chrome combination locks. The air tastes of stale coffee.

He re-wraps my ankles with duct tape, forces me into a folding chair and binds my legs and my chest to the seat frame. When Rags is finished, I look like The Silver Mummy.

"Don't go anywhere," he says. "Ha."

He types more numbers on the keypad, then leaves through the double steel doors, no doubt to hunt wild Arnolds. Though my head aches and the overhead lights glare like the noon sunshine in Mexico, I take comfort. At least I have a chance. Arnold extricated himself from the car, and my new pal at the D.A.'s office could be on a pay phone right this minute, calling for help.

I hear two gunshots. They're outside, muffled by those steel doors. Chances are it was my former sales manager Rags doing the shooting, but maybe Arnold turned a trick on him. He's a cop, right? A Federal officer. Why couldn't he wrestle that semiautomatic away from a former stockbroker?

Another possibility, Arnold used a hidden cell phone to call the Piscataway cops, a rescue squad that has already arrived and just nailed Rags twice with their Glock nines.

The steel entrance thrusts open. Rags limps in, dragging the non-ambulatory Arnold Casey. Fresh blood colors the front of Arnold's white shirt.

TWENTY-NINE

Mostly we humans are delusional about dying. We pretend death will never choose us, that fatal disease and natural misfortune only conclude the lives of others. Both as a society and as individuals our time is far less productive when we worry about death, so maybe the fantasy is nature's way of supporting us. But make no mistake, delusion it is. Nobody gets out alive.

Watching Rags haul my bleeding hero Federal Officer Arnold into Aunt Lena's break room certainly penetrates *my* mortality armor. The flaming crash landing my ex-wife Susan always predicted for me seems on final approach. I can smell the smoke.

Rags once again slices the duct tape binding my ankles, makes a fist of my shirt. "You're going to drag Arnold to the elevator for me," Rags says. "Turn around, open your palms and squat."

Rags should have carried a semiautomatic when he was sales manager. If not friends, at least we could have had a working relationship based on mutual respect.

My ex-sales manager puts Arnold's jacket collar in my duct-taped hands. Arnold of course is still inside the jacket. The man is heavy, too. I'm forced to drag him toward the elevator, past the last vending machine. It's tough going. I don't have the best grip. Plus I can't lean far enough to properly balance.

Wonder how much Beth and Ryan will miss me when I'm gone. I know Luis will be sorry he has no one to lecture about questionable morals. One good thing, Arnold isn't dead. He groaned twice so far on the drag over here, probably from being towed across the floor like a sack of onions. The blood trail he deposits isn't as thick as it was. He must be pressing on the wound. At the vending machines, my legs cramp. I stumble, sink to my knees and let loose of Arnold's collar.

Rags aims the semiautomatic at my teeth. "Get up."

Scary thing, that black hole. Makes you think about brain electronics, chemical connections and reflexes—like, will I hear or feel the shot? I force myself to carry Arnold the last five yards to the elevator. Rags hits the call button. We're in a narrow corridor, the employee's locker and break space one of many intersecting rooms along the hall's length.

The elevator arrives. Double sliding doors open. Rags makes me reload Arnold in my behind-the-back grip, tug him inside until my forehead bumps the back of the elevator. Rags punches THIRD FLOOR, then CLOSE. Old elevator buttons can take a few seconds, but this one works instantly.

I might try something with that.

On the third floor, when Rags asks me to, I make a show of needing room to drag Arnold out of the elevator. I bump into Rags' broken leg, stomp on his foot. He smacks me with the gun, but finally shifts outside the doorway to give me room. I drop Arnold in the nice blue suit, catch Rags by surprise with a hard kick into the hallway, then bump the FIRST FLOOR and CLOSE buttons with my forehead.

I spin sideways to make myself a smaller target as the doors shut.

Instead of lunging for the rubber-tipped bumpers to halt us, Rags fires his weapon at the closing steel curtain. The bullet slams the inside wall of the elevator, passing within six inches of my chest. Hot powder and residue brush my neck as the doors bang shut. Rags screams and kicks as we lurch downward.

"Nice move, pal," Arnold says. He sits up and shows me his back. "The key to my handcuffs is in my left ass pocket."

Arnold in the nice blue suit is not only talking, he no longer acts badly injured.

"Hey, Carr," Arnold says. "Move it!"

His quick recovery and the loud voice startle me. Not to mention me kicking Rags and almost getting shot. I'm confused. I have to remember Arnold is a Federal officer, a trained warrior in the battle against—

"If you want to live," Arnold says. "Get these cuffs off me."

Okay, now I'm back.

Arnold winces when I roll him over, but I easily find the key in his pocket. It's much more of a struggle to unlock his handcuffs with my hands still taped together. "I thought you were dying," I say.

"Hit the emergency STOP button."

Well okay, Dick Tracy. Again with my forehead, I punch a red, round button the size of a fifty-cent piece. Our elevator rattles to a halt. Blinking red lights indicate our troubled condition. We're stuck above the first floor, well past the second. My forehead hurts.

When I finally get the cuffs off him, Arnold tries to stand up. He can't, staggers instead, the knees not working. Too weak, he drops back to elevator floor. "Sit down with me and turn your back," he says. "Let's get that tape off you."

His hands work quickly.

"How badly are you wounded?" I say.

"The bullet went through shoulder muscle," he says. "It didn't hit a bone which is good. A paper towel in the wound slowed the bleeding." Arnold pulls the last of the tape from my wrists. "But I've lost some blood. I'm dizzy and weak."

"What are we going to do?" I say.

"Tell me you have a cell phone," Arnold says.

"Sorry. Rags took it."

"Do you know where we are?"

"Aunt Lena's Cookie factory," I say.

"Where is that? What town?"

"Piscataway. It's where Rags works. He's the night janitor."

"Then he'll know how to shut the phones off, probably has a key to get this elevator moving again. We have to get ready."

Arnold tears his shirt and I kneel to help. He shows me how to wrap his wound with material, fashioning a makeshift bandage to keep on the pressure. We use the tape off my wrists to secure the dressing.

"Anything we do is risky," Arnold says, "but I think our best shot is to go back to the third floor, look for a phone or a place to hide. People will come looking for me in a few hours."

"But the third floor is where Rags is," I say.

"I'd expect him to run down the stairs to meet us," Arnold says. "But you know him better than me—you think he'd stay up there, wait for us to double back?"

Interesting question. Reminds me of my high school pitching career, standing out on the mound, wondering if the batter was expecting a fastball or a curve. In this situation, I'd say—as usual—Rags is mostly likely searching for his ass, and therefore on the move. I release the STOP button and poke THIRD FLOOR.

It's a hell ride. The elevator at Aunt Lena's Piscataway cookie factory becomes my personal version of "The Lady or the Tiger." Sure, there are three floors instead of two doors, so my odds are fifty-percent better than the guy in that famous short story. But I share the same heart-pounding dilemma: Which hides the tiger? Trickles of sweat slide down my ribcage.

"Stand me up," Arnold says.

I bend to clasp Arnold's outstretched hands. His palms are clammy. His cheeks and neck glow paper white. The bandage we put together already leaks blood. I pull him onto his feet, lean him against the back elevator wall as gently as I can. He totters, knees and legs not wanting to support him. I clasp his middle until he catches his balance.

"Ow," Arnold says. "Gunshots hurt."

"First time you've been shot?"

"First time for anybody in my particular D.A. unit," he says. "We're pencil pushers."

"Insider trading cases?"

"How'd you guess?"

Our elevator approaches floor number three. Arnold has me help him into the opposite corner, points for me to stay at the controls. The elevator's floor space is four feet wider than the doors. With Arnold and me spread on either of the doorways like goalposts, we'll be out of the line of fire when the steel box opens.

"If you see Ragsdale, punch the CLOSE DOOR button," Arnold says. "If I see him, I'll say *hit it.*"

General Schwarzkopf he's not, but I don't have a better plan.

The elevator doors part on the third floor. I can't see anything but stacks of cylindrical cardboard food containers and a red hand-truck big enough to deliver a small car. I glance at Arnold. He shakes his head, doesn't see Rags either.

I grab the elevator door to prevent it from closing. Arnold bravely sticks his head out, peeks both directions. "It's like we thought," he says. "Ragsdale ran downstairs." He pulls his face back inside. "Hit emergency STOP again."

At my command, the elevator jiggles and halts. I stare at Arnold, awaiting further instructions. Instinctively I trust this guy, trust him like I do Luis. Well, almost. I wouldn't tell Arnold how much and when I knew about that Fishman Corp. merger.

"You have to do it," Arnold says. "I can't."

"Do what?"

"Get one of those round food containers on that hand-truck, bring it back here to keep the elevator from moving."

"I can do that," I say, "but won't Rags come up the stairs and shoot us?"

"Maybe," Arnold says. "But we'll know where he's coming from. Besides, his plan was never to shoot you or he already would have done it."

"He tried."

"Yeah, but he really wants to torture you."

THIRTY

If Rags wants to torture me, Arnold Casey of the New York District Attorney's Office says, "That gives us something to work with. He needs to capture you alive. Now get a feel for that red hand-truck—it's bigger than anything you've used—then if you can, bring one of those cylindrical containers over here to the elevator."

On my mission, I notice the third floor isn't really a floor—not a solid one anyway. I'm walking and driving the hand-truck on black steel mesh, a see-through grid that goes everywhere in and around a dozen stainless steel domes. Like half-protruding silver eggs, domes peek through round holes in the mesh across the whole floor. Since we're visiting Aunt Lena's Cookie factory this evening, I'm thinking these big shiny eggs could be mixing vats.

Another passenger jet out of Newark rattles the roof. The hanging mesh walkway—the floor—vibrates and sways. Nice. Supporting the black mesh I'm walking on are hundreds of twenty-foot-long steel rods attached to the ceiling with nuts and bolts. Not exactly the Rock of Gibraltar.

Arnold was right about the hand-truck. It has electronic controls and a place to stand. Strictly for factories. But mounted on four automobile wheels, the bulky cart scoots around easily. Only two control sticks—forward, reverse, and left, right. That's my kind of cockpit. I load a pallet with a two-hundred-gallon container of corn syrup in two minutes.

"Right here," Arnold says.

He helps me position my cargo half in the elevator, half on the mesh floor. When we're finished, the elevator doors can't close, even if Rags has a special key.

"Now what?" I say.

"Did you see the stairway?"

"Over there."

"Only the one?"

"Think so. That's all I saw."

"Okay, then move a container or two to the stairs," Arnold says. "If you can, lay the barrels on their side when you get there, roll them to the edge of the stairway."

I'm getting the picture. "But not too close, right? We don't want Rags to see it when he comes barging up."

"You'd better hurry," Arnold says.

I'm hiding behind two-hundred-gallon cardboard drums of African chocolate, shipped from the Ivory Coast to Guadalajara, Mexico, where according to the labels and shipping papers, the chocolate was battered and beaten into chips. I intend to hand deliver these mega-size packages momentarily.

I left Arnold inside the elevator, propped against the container we used to block the doors. Arnold's taken a turn for the worse. If he doesn't get medical help soon, I'm afraid he'll fall unconscious, or worse. I covered his chest with a mover's blanket I found beside the hand-truck. He could be slipping into shock.

The sound of limping footsteps on the stairway gooses my heart rate. Rags is coming, three-legging it onto the second-floor landing. I count to three, then lean my weight into the first of two giant cardboard cans. The African chocolate groans and begins to roll. Here, Rags. Catch this. My special delivery shakes the building and fills the stairwell with booming, crashing noise. Hope the warning comes too late for Rags.

I scamper to the edge, see Rags leap back to the second-floor landing and jump down an instant before my rolling can of whip-ass slams into the landing wall. Missed. The structure of the building shudders. The container breaks open, spilling chocolate chips all over the second floor landing and the tip of Rags' crutch.

He sees me watching, aims his semiautomatic at me.

There's yellow fire burning the muzzle of Rags' weapon. Hornets buzz my head. Three explosions make me dive backward. My ribs skid on the steel mesh floor, but I pick myself up, haul ass back to Arnold. I need his expertise.

"Hey, Arnold," I say. "I've been counting Rags' shots. Four at Luis' place, two downstairs, one in the elevator, three or four more on the stairs. That's ten or eleven shots. Shouldn't he be out of ammunition?"

The white collar crime expert flutters his eyelids. "You missed him with the chocolate?"

"Lucky bastard."

"Can you move the container, get the elevator going?"

"No. I left the hand-truck by the stairs. Rags will be here in seconds."

Arnold sighs. My hope that murderous Rags is out of bullets is all I have left. There's no place to hide, and I wouldn't leave Arnold. The man kept me alive.

"Ten shots is a lot, right?" I say.

"His gun is a Sig Sauer," Arnold says. His voice is an out-of-breath whisper. "Many models offer ten or twelve shots. His could have as many as seventeen."

"Seventeen?"

Rags' feet bang on the mesh flooring not far away. He's on our third level, running directly toward us. I tuck Arnold as far behind container of chocolate as possible. "Seventeen shots?" I say. "What is it, a machine gun?"

Rags' pounding feet reach the elevator.

"A law enforcement model," Arnold says.

The man knows his guns. I crouch against the container, hoping the first thing I see is Rags' Sig Sauer. I'll try to grab it.

Rags whacks me with his crutch and hurries past, drops his back against the elevator wall. His gun is aimed at my center. "It's called a P229SCT," Rags says. "Seventeen rounds per magazine for the nine-millimeter version."

I lift my hands.

Rags leans closer. "Even comes with a night vision sight."

I see the blow coming, but not in time. Rags' fancy Sig Sauer busts the side of my head.

* * *

I wake up dizzy and cold inside a perfect blackness. My arms and shoulders are stretched painfully behind me, my spine flat pressed against a hard, knobby surface. My hands are bound tightly at the wrist. What the hell?

"Aus-tin."

The high-pitched, squeaky voice sounds evil, but in a silly, over-done way, a disguise meant to scare me. It's working, though. Being tied up in the dark is something less than reassuring. I imagine this screechy creature—has to be Rags— in a long white coat, with sharp knives. Preparing tools in a stainless steel operating room. My head throbs from the gun smack Rags gave me. Odd that he altered his voice.

Dr. Squeaky says, "I know you have a reputation for a fancy mouth."

The voice's contrived tones buzz around my head like angry wasps. Rags must have some kind of electronic vocal distorter. The way the sound resonates on my clothes and skin, it makes me imagine I'm confined inside a huge, polished container.

Dr. Squeaky says, "You're not talking your way out of this one."

Mama Bones stops laughing and clicks the switch. This megaphone Gianni found is more fun than a barrel of monkey wrenches. She figures she is scaring the pants off poor Austin. Why not? Tommy Ragsdale would already have made mincemeat of him if she and Gianni hadn't appeared. She leans over the big silver egg, megaphone on. "How's that full-boat grin now, huh?"

Gianni showed her how to set the controls on super high-frequency distortion mode. Mama Bones giggles every time she hears her voice come out. She sounds like a crazy cartoon mouse. Wonder why playing tricks on Austin is so much fun?

"Someone's conked me on the head, tied me to a post," Austin says. "Wasn't you, was it?"

Mama Bones giggles through the megaphone. "For your information, that's not a post you're tied to. That's a gigantic mixing blade, one of four inside that industrial dough-maker."

"Dough-maker?" he says.

Mama Bones hears noises, like Gianni and the boys finally cornered that crazy Tommy Ragsdale. She hopes he still has the real ruby.

More funny noises from outside as she lifts the lid on the dough-mixer. Running feet, clinks and clacks, shouting. Maybe she's going too far with her joke, scaring poor Austin. But she couldn't resist, not when she figured out what Tommy Ragsdale planned to do to Austin at the bakery.

"You and I are going to make cookies," she says. "Stockbroker chip."

The huge lid on the dough-mixer lifts full open. Light washes away the dark as I hear two or three odd *clinks*. A face appears. *Hell,* no. It's Mama Bones. Her hawkish features peer at me. How did she get here?

"Gianni's gonna find that Big Mojo ruby any minute," Mama Bones says. "Then I send him down there to untie you."

"You mean this is a joke? You're not really going to grind me up into cookie dough?"

"Of course not. You got a big mouth, but you're not a bad guy. I'm not even going to kill Tommy Ragsdale, the jerk who used to beat up my granddaughter. Him, we'll turn over to the police."

Muscles relax all over my body. This steel tube doesn't seem as cold.

"Tell me, smarty pants—while I'm waiting to hear from Gianni—are you still in love with that redhead, Patricia Willis?"

"Since the day after Luis' wedding. We went for a walk on the beach."

"Ha. It was my magic, that perfume you sniffed on my neck at the wedding. You were supposed to fall in love with Luis' new bride, but the redhead jumped in, smooched you first."

"Sorry, Mama Bones, but it was chemistry."

"That's right—cranberry pits and bat balls. And by the way, so you know, me and Gianni are going to keep the ruby when we find it."

"It belongs to Vic, of course."

"No, he gave it to that slut. She lost it. Me and Gianni gonna find it and keep it, and you're not going to tell Vic or the redhead nothing, right?"

"No way." I know Mama Bones said she was going to release me, but perhaps it would be a smart idea to further cultivate her friendship. As long as I'm still down here tied up inside a giant cookie dough mixer. "Tell me where Gianni caught Rags, maybe I can figure out where he stashed the ruby," I say. "You know me, Mama Bones, I'm a pretty smart guy. And I know Rags."

"You know Tommy Ragsdale so well, smarty pants, tell me why he put a bug in my Vic's office if he was already in cahoots with Mallory?"

"You have it wrong," I say. "Rags heard everything on his listening device, but Mallory figured him out, followed him and was outside Patricia's when Rags shot Vic. Mallory muscled in on Rags with all that info. And it was Mallory who knew Patricia Willis from way back."

"Every man in Seaside County knew her."

"So where did you catch Rags tonight?" I ask.

"Gianni chased him outside, in the back. Rags has some kinda machine gun. They're still out there, by the loading dock. He's finally out of ammo."

A sound comes back to me, the *clinks* as Mama Bones opened the dough mixer. The second or third one reminded me of a wrench, or maybe hail, dropping on a tin roof.

"Let me ask you, Mama Bones, am I inside a mixer near the back of the building? Maybe close to an open back window?"

"Yeah? How you know that, huh?"

"I think I know where your ruby is."

THIRTY-ONE

While she and Gianni check out my suggested location, Mama Bones is nice enough to leave the big dough-mixer's lid up so I can keep a close eye on these knobby, geared blades. The way the edges fit together, I figure death wouldn't be *quite* instantaneous. Just enough ripping action to make hellish pain my last taste of earth.

Sure hope they find the ruby, or spinel. I know Mama Bones said she was going to let me out of here, but I'd like that to happen as soon as possible. Sooner even. You never know with Mama Bones.

Mama Bones walks a shuffle I've known for years, ever since I started dialing for dollars at the old Shore Securities with her son, Mr. Vic. The grated mesh floor changes the tone, but I hear that familiar scuffle rhythm now, like I did when she used to visit the office.

"Well, what do you know, smarty pants," Mama Bones says. "You were right. Gianni got a ladder, picked up the ruby and the glass fake on his first pass over the loading dock roof."

"That's wonderful, Mama Bones," I say. "Fantastic. Can I get out of here?"

"They were both right where you said."

"Yup, tin roofs make sounds like no other. So that's a big score for you and Gianni. Let's go celebrate. I'll buy. Come on, get me out of here and we'll—"

"I no think so."

My stomach fills with lead. "Why not? You promised. And then I found the ruby."

"Lies are part of my nature," she says. "I think of them as business exaggerations."

Blood drains from my face. "I can keep my mouth shut. About everything, honest."

"I no think so."

"Mama Bones, please. Remember how much you liked my kids when you met them at Luis'?"

"Sure. Beautiful. And I really owe you big time for the tip on the ruby. Saved us hours. But I think you got this coming, Austin Carr. My son says you swiped his business and stole his girl."

"Jeez, Mama Bones, how many women does one man need. He's married. Oh, Mama Bones, you're kidding me, right? This is another joke?"

She cackles. "Yeah, I'm sorry. But maybe you could do me one more favor, huh? I just thought of something besides not telling Vic and the redhead about me finding the ruby. One more little promise before I get Gianni to pull you out of there."

"A promise?"

"Sure. A little one. A promise and a favor. Maybe two. Then you're all set."

No one in Branchtown asks me what happened, how I got the scar on my face, or the double vision which will slowly go away weeks later. No one asks me why my name is coming down off the front of my business. No one asks because everyone knows.

"All right, this stockholders meeting is officially called to order," I say.

"How come you don't try my coffee, mister smarty pants big shot?"

I ignore Mama Bones. She knows very well why I will never consume another drop of any food or beverage she prepares. "I've already handed out the minutes from the last meeting, and today's agenda," I say. "Are there any questions or old items before we discuss today's new business?"

"Yeah, I gotta question," Mama Bones says. "How come a guy like you—investigated by the Federal police, an inside trader, involved in the assault of a Federal officer—how come a guy like you is our chairman, huh?"

I give Mama Bones a cold stare. "It's about the stock, Mama Bones. My percentage of the company versus your son's? Fifty-one-percent means *whatever* we vote on, I win. Do you want to vote on who's chairman?"

Arnold Casey and I both got lucky. We not only survived, but came through our battle with Rags largely intact. Tom Ragsdale has pleaded guilty to three attempted murders and will spend years in prison. Jim Mallory must have left town. No one has seen him since that night on Sandy Hook. Thanks to his ever present bullet-proof vest, Santo Vargas is sore but unharmed, back in Las Vegas. And sadly, Patricia Willis and I have parted ways. Real love or fake love, we were there for a while, but something snapped for both of us not long after that last night as Luis'.

"I gotta ask another question," Mama Bones says. "How come our new black and gold electric sign out front with Vic's name isn't as big as the last one, the sign with *your* name, huh?"

I should explain. I'm not President, Chairman of the Board and majority owner of Carr Securities anymore. I'm President, Chairman of the Board, and majority owner of V. Bonacelli Investment Corp.—this in honor of my friend, junior partner, the soon-to-be-recovered Mr. Vic. As another favor I promised Mama Bones—to keep from being ground into hamburger—I've agreed to sell Mr. Vic ten ownership points of my current fifty-one, effectively giving Vic control again. This is set to happen one year from now.

"It's a new city zoning regulation," I say. "Branchtown's city fathers want smaller signs. They're going for up-market shoppers now."

Thanks to Mr. Vic, who handed out his power of attorney for representation on our board to his mother, looks like I'll have a meddlesome new voice hawking me at these stockholders meetings while I finish up as chairman.

"Zoning regulations, my butt," Mama Bones says. "Mayor what's-his-name is a friend of mine. I'm gonna have a talk with him Sunday at church."

At least I own controlling interest for another year, and maybe we can make enough money during that time to educate my children. Most importantly, thanks to Mama

Bones not throwing the switch on the dough machine, at least I am above ground and in one piece.

I might stay this way if I don't drink her coffee.

Six-thirty sharp the next Monday, Randall Zimmer, Esquire picks me up at my condo in a chauffeured black Lincoln limousine. Inside the plush carriage, there's Starbucks coffee, pastries, juice, and muffins, but Mr. Z warns me to save room for a "more substantial" breakfast in the city.

Barring extra-bad traffic on the way to Manhattan, he says, we're doing The Plaza coffee shop with our hot shot gunslinger from Washington. This newest member of the Austin Carr Defense Team, an expert in securities cases, Thomas Britain, "is *the* man to have with us today," Mr. Z assures me, an "old pro who's won dozens of major insider trading cases" and has a "special personal interest."

After I am coaxed into an enthusiastic response, and post-facto agreement, Mr. Z informs me that Thomas Britain charges eight hundred dollars per hour, and Britain's clock started last night when his wife drove him to Dulles International Airport.

"Sure we need him?" I say.

In the back seat of our black limo, headed for my doomsday interview with the U.S. District Attorney for New York, Mr. Zimmer peels the paper off a banana-walnut muffin. "Do you want to go to jail?"

"Uh...no." I hate banana anything. In fact, I don't care for muffins period. They're too healthy. Give me lots of sugar, butter, and animal fat on my breakfast menu.

"Do you want to lose your company and your Series Seven securities license?"

"*Hell*, no. I'll end up selling used cars."

"Do you want to pay a fine of, say double the quarter-million-plus profit made in your account?"

"Silly question, Mr. Z."

Zimmer breaks the muffin in half. He's about to give me his final word on the subject.

"Then don't worry about the hourly rate on Britain. Be glad we *know* Thomas Britain. Be glad he's *available*."

I nod. "Okay. If you say so. I bow to your superior intellect and specific knowledge of all things legal."

"Good. Then we'll go over your story again at breakfast with Britain, confirm the specific information you'll need to work into your answers."

By story, Mr. Z means my *new* story. The truth about Mr. Vic hacking my account would land me in jail.

My lawyer says, "I'll pick up the tab for breakfast."

THIRTY-TWO

In the U.S. District Attorney's conference room, Thomas Britain, Mr. Z and I line up on one side of an oblong table the length of a Carnival Cruise liner. Across from us are; one, a very young-looking District Attorney, John something; two, his blond female assistant; and three, a couple of Securities and Exchange Commission officials, Humpty and Dumpty. One SEC investigator is a male, the other a woman, but they both wear dull brown suits over tall frames, and both wear tortoise shell glasses.

An unpadded steel chair grinds against my butt and shoulders. The U.S. District Attorney for New York rests in soft leather. Silence has filled the room for two or three full minutes while he read. When the D.A. glances up from his papers and stares at me, drops of sweat roll down my flanks.

"Hi, Tom," the D.A says. "I haven't seen you in a while."

Not Humpty, Dumpty or yours truly have a clue to whom the D.A. is talking. Does he have my name mixed up? Who's Tom, I'm thinking. When the D.A. shifts his eyes to my newly acquired, high-priced mouthpiece from Washington, I remember. Oh, yeah. Thomas Britain.

Tom says, "Haven't seen you since last Christmas, I think it was, John. I know it was just before your dad and I went fishing in Venezuela last January."

John the D.A. nods, apparently remembering with fondness his Christmas with my parachute attorney from Washington. John the handsome D.A. can't be out of law school more than a year or three. He looks Irish Catholic with the dark hair and green eyes. Probably a name like O'Connor or Fennell. I wasn't listening. My palms are too sweaty.

"Your dad told me to say hi, by the way," my attorney Thomas Britain says to John the D.A. "I talked to him yesterday about a charity dinner we're putting together."

"Something to do with Harvard, no doubt," the D.A. says.

"A new sports facility."

Silence once more grips the conference room. I might not be the only one unnerved by this cozy relationship. Slowly, the young D.A. gazes at each of us, even the SEC team on his side of the table. He's poised and authoritative, unusually so for his youth. I can see why John the D.A. is going places in politics. Well, that and rich friends like my attorney, Thomas Britain.

"Tom and my father went to school together," the D.A. announces.

Duh. I have to say Mr. Eight-Hundred-An-Hour, Mr. Harvard Graduate, Mr. Right Man For The Job, Sir Thomas Britain, certainly earned his fee here. Does Mr. Z know how to hire consultants, or what? Be glad he's available, Mr. Z said. Wow, talk about your Old Boy Network...fishing in Venezuela with the D.A.'s father...I think I'm going to be sick.

After I stand up and cheer.

"All right, Mr. Carr," the D.A. says. "Why don't we begin by you telling us a little about yourself...your background...schools. How you became a stockbroker."

I start with a full-boat grin.

At breakfast, Mr. Z assured me Thomas Ragsdale was not now, nor ever had been on the D.A.'s radar, so I shouldn't worry about the D.A. owning a tape of Patricia's story and my following conversations. Not that it would matter, because I stick to the truth, right through the part where Patricia mentions her brother, what he did for a living, and how he knew the merger was coming. I tell them everything.

At this point—rather convincingly, I think—I explain to the young D.A., his even younger and prettier blond assistant and the two SEC officials, that I considered Patricia Willis's story merely a tip, not inside information. I didn't believe her attorney brother would ever divulge such details to anyone.

I back up this assertion with several important facts.

"I'm a stockbroker," I say. "If I knew this Fishman Corp. was a sure thing, why didn't I score points with my biggest clients, put them all in the stock? I didn't. Not one. And why didn't I cash in my two kids' college funds. They're small amounts, but another nine thousand dollars would have bought a lot of options."

These are the points Zimmer and Britain told me to make while we ate breakfast at The Plaza this morning. As instructed, I wait for the right moment and slip these facts into the conversation, not in a prearranged speech.

I never say a word about Mr. Vic being the one to load up my account. If that's lying, or misdirection, I don't care. I truly did nothing wrong.

Later in the Lincoln limo, after we've packed off Sir Thomas Britain for the airport and driven back to Jersey, my attorney and I take a minute at my condo's curb to make our goodbyes.

"Unless they turn up something new," Mr. Z says, "I believe you're off the hook."

"Really?"

"Yes. You weren't the target before, and you gave them no reason today to change their minds. The Fed's civil and criminal investigations are both focused on Las Vegas, even more so after today. The Vegas people are the ones who made the big money."

"Think I'll keep my firm and my license?"

"It certainly looks like it."

"And the illegal three hundred grand profit in my account...should I make out the check to the SEC, or the U.S. Treasury?"

"Hang on. Let me make everything perfectly clear," he says.

Mr. Z reaches between us, taps a series of numbers on a keypad in the backseat console. "I've been worried since you had me draw up those change in ownership papers for Carr Securities."

The console splits and a secret side compartment opens. "The Bonacellis have a history of small business failures, fraud, bad dealing and worse," he says. "So as a precaution, I used that Limited Power of Attorney you signed to close your account with them."

"But that's *my* firm."

"Yes, but you've agreed to sell controlling interest. I thought it best to move your assets, especially since Mr. Bonacelli might think he deserves a share."

"A share of what?"

From the secret compartment, Mr. Z pulls a plain white envelope. I swear my attorney wears a full-boat grin. "I don't think you understand, Austin. You're off the hook. The D.A. and the SEC are done with the Austin Carr portion of this investigation."

"You mean..."

"The trades and profit in your account are not illegal. You'll be allowed to keep every single penny—less short-term capital gains and state income taxes, of course. And here it is, ready for you to deposit in a new account somewhere."

Mr. Z hands me a cashier's check for three hundred forty-two thousand six hundred fifty-one dollars and forty-seven cents.

Looks like Beth and Ryan will be going to any school they want.

ABOUT THE AUTHOR

Former Los Angeles Times reporter Jack Getze is Fiction Editor for Anthony nominated Spinetingler Magazine. Through the Los Angeles Times/Washington Post News Syndicate, his news and feature stories have been published in over five-hundred newspapers and periodicals worldwide. His screwball mysteries, BIG NUMBERS and BIG MONEY, were first published by Hilliard Harris in 2007 and 2008. His short stories have appeared in *A Twist of Noir* and *Beat to a Pulp*. He is an Active Member of Mystery Writers of America's New York Chapter.

http://austincarrscrimediary.blogspot.com/

OTHER TITLES FROM DOWN AND OUT BOOKS

See www.DownAndOutBooks.com for complete list

By J.L. Abramo
Catching Water in a Net
Clutching at Straws
Counting to Infinity
Gravesend
Chasing Charlie Chan
Circling the Runway (*)

By Trey R. Barker
2,000 Miles to Open Road
Road Gig: A Novella
Exit Blood

By Richard Barre
The Innocents
Bearing Secrets
Christmas Stories
The Ghosts of Morning
Blackheart Highway
Burning Moon
Echo Bay
Lost

By Rob Brunet
Stinking Rich

By Milton T. Burton
Texas Noir

By Reed Farrel Coleman
The Brooklyn Rules

By Tom Crowley
Vipers Tail
Murder in the Slaughterhouse

By Frank De Blase
Pine Box for a Pin-Up
Busted Valentines and Other Dark Delights
The Cougar's Kiss (*)

By Les Edgerton
The Genuine, Imitation, Plastic Kidnapping

By A.C. Frieden
Tranquility Denied
The Serpent's Game

By Jack Getze
Big Numbers
Big Money
Big Mojo

By Keith Gilman
Bad Habits

(*)—Coming Soon

OTHER TITLES FROM DOWN AND OUT BOOKS

See www.DownAndOutBooks.com for complete list

By Terry Holland
An Ice Cold Paradise
Chicago Shiver

By Darrel James, Linda O. Johnston
& Tammy Kaehler (editors)
Last Exit to Murder

By David Housewright
& Renée Valois
The Devil and the Diva

By David Housewright
Finders Keepers
Full House

By Jon Jordan
Interrogations

By Jon & Ruth Jordan (editors)
Murder and Mayhem in Muskego

By Bill Moody
Czechmate
The Man in Red Square
Solo Hand
The Death of a Tenor Man
The Sound of the Trumpet
Bird Lives!

By Gary Phillips
The Perpetrators
Scoundrels (Editor)
Treacherous

By Gary Phillips, Tony Chavira
& Manoel Maglhaes
Beat L.A. (Graphic Novel)

By Robert J. Randisi
Upon My Soul
Souls of the Dead
Envy the Dead (*)

By Lono Waiwaiole
Wiley's Lament
Wiley's Shuffle
Wiley's Refrain
Dark Paradise

By Vincent Zandri
Moonlight Weeps

(*)—Coming Soon